BE MY GUEST

BE MY GUEST

Caroline Clemmons

Five Star • Waterville, Maine

Published in 2004 in conjunction with The Ferguson
Literary Agency.

The text of this edition is unabridged.

Set in 11 pt. Plantin by Ramona Watson.

Printed in the United States on permanent paper.

ISBN 1-59414-141-X (hc : alk. paper)

To my husband, who is always my hero, with thanks for encouraging me to write. And to my father, who gave me a love for reading.

And thanks to my family, to Mary Adair, Carol Rose Doss, Victoria Chancellor, Diane Ernst, Warren Norwood, Carol Roberts, and to the group at NTRWA for encouragement and support.

Prologue

"Kelly, I don't want to talk about it." Will Harrison sat with a small saddle balanced between his right leg and the kitchen table. His left leg, entirely in a cast, stretched out before him. His left foot rested on a kitchen chair. The saddle, once treasured by his wife and her mother before her, now belonged to his daughter. Though lovingly cared for all its years, the aging leather now required mending.

Kelly threw her arms around his neck. "Daddy, please think about it." She gave her father a loud kiss on his cheek. "After all, Mommy wouldn't want you to be all alone forever."

Will sighed. "I'm not alone, punkin'. I have you." His reassuring words weren't exactly true. Many nights he lay awake long past midnight, unable to quiet the hollow, lonely ache that had become a part of him when Nancy died. Would this pain be with him for the rest of his life? He reminded himself those thoughts served no purpose. Best to concentrate on the saddle and his feisty daughter.

"Daddy, when I go away to college, you really will be alone. I don't want to worry about you here all by yourself while I'm trying to study."

Will stopped mending and raised his head to look at his daughter, a mixture of amusement and exasperation on his face. "Kelly, you're ten years old. I believe I have a few years yet before you go off to college. Besides, I have your Aunt Lori Beth and Uncle Tommy Joe, and Grandma, and Aunt Rose, and Lily here and her family."

He glanced at the housekeeper standing at the kitchen counter. As she slid a dish into the dishwasher, Lily Chapas flashed Will a look that told him he would get neither support nor sympathy from her on this issue.

"But Daddy-y-y," Kelly pleaded. "You need to date a woman and then get married again. If you take your wedding ring off, a nice lady will want to date you."

"Kelly Marie Harrison, the subject is closed." Will pulled so hard he almost broke the leather lace he was threading through the saddle cover.

Kelly knew his patience was wearing thin when her father used her full name, yet she could not resist one more try.

"Please, promise me you'll at least think about asking a nice lady for a date. Oh, please, please, please." She stood in front of him, a pitiful look on her face and hands clasped together as she pleaded.

Will stopped his work on the saddle. His daughter knew just how to get around him. With a resigned grin, he acquiesced. "Okay, we'll make a deal. I promise to think—that's just *think* about it, mind you—if you promise to stop talking about this dating thing."

How could his little girl change so fast? It seemed only yesterday her conversation centered on horses and dolls. How much did she actually understand about dating and—related topics?

He felt inadequate, and he hated this talk in which they seemed endlessly involved. "If I ever meet a woman who interests me, I'll ask her out. In the meantime, you are *not* ever to mention it again. Is that a deal?"

Kelly's ponytail switched back and forth as she hopped in glee. "Oh, thank you, Daddy. And promise you'll think about taking off the ring, too. That way, when you meet someone nice, she won't think you're married."

He held up a hand to halt her speech. "I'll take off the ring *if* I meet someone who interests me. Now are you happy?"

She kissed his cheek again loudly and gave his shoulders a hug. "Oh, yes. I just know you'll find me a new mother if you look. I can hardly wait."

Will sighed. He didn't even know where to start looking. . . .

Chapter One

The dashboard clock displayed one o'clock when Aurora turned off U.S. Highway 84 to drive into Snyder. Clouds gathered and rumbled with thunder over the West Texas town. Aurora's empty stomach rumbled with them. Fatigue and apprehension overshadowed her usually cheerful nature. She passed every one of the usual fast food places before she spotted a family restaurant. Unfortunately, cars and trucks filled the parking lot to capacity. Aurora scowled.

Then someone's tail lights glowed and a car backed out of the prime parking slot in front of the restaurant entrance. Aurora saw the lone man in the dusty red pickup truck facing her waiting for the space. Exhausted and hungry, she decided suddenly not to be polite about it and she zipped her blue Mustang into the vacated slot before the less maneuverable truck could occupy the space.

She heard the truck horn honk and saw the look of irritation on the face of its driver as she got out of her car. With an impish smile, she blew him a kiss before she hurried into the restaurant. After all, any *real* gentleman would have given me the only parking spot in the first place, she told herself to ease her nagging conscience.

Her conscience would not be quieted so easily. She must be far more tired and worried than she realized. Never had she acted so rudely. Regretting her impetuous actions already, she felt thankful the exchange occurred with a stranger and not someone she might meet again.

Seated in the corner booth, Aurora ordered a hamburger, french fries, and a large soda. While she waited for her food, she reviewed the local attractions in and around the town of Snyder in her Texas guidebook. Suddenly, she sensed someone standing beside her booth. As she looked up—and up—a huge cowboy with most of his left leg in a cast leaned his crutches against the side of the booth. He slid onto the seat beside her, which pinned her in the booth with him.

Aurora scooted to the right as far as possible. "Hey, who do you think you are? This is my booth, and you certainly haven't been invited to share it with me!"

"Your car's sitting in my parking space, Ma'am. I thought I'd sit in your booth," he said calmly as he removed his pearl gray Stetson and ran his fingers through his hair. He turned in his seat to hang the hat on the hook at the end of the booth by his crutches.

Aurora blushed when she realized that this was the man whose parking space she had mischievously stolen. He must have had to park a long way from the door and hobble in on those crutches. Oh, no. This was embarrassing. The one time in her life she'd deliberately acted rudely, her victim turned out to be a man on crutches. Still, he had his nerve sitting beside her without so much as a "may I."

Her chin came up defensively. "Okay, I apologize. If you used one of those disability placards on your rear view mirror, people would know you had a problem."

"Lady, my problem is that you stole my spot," he said coolly. He lifted his left leg so his cast-encased foot rested on the seat facing them, then swiveled his torso so he could look directly at her.

Aurora smelled the cowboy's aftershave mixed with the clean scent of his breath when he turned his face toward

11

her. His stone gray eyes met hers. She saw anger drain from his eyes, replaced by stunned amazement. He leaned toward her.

Blood surged through her body and her awakened senses rocketed into response. She felt the softness of his blue chambray shirt sleeve, which brushed against her arm. For a moment she had the astonishing thought that this cowboy might lean further toward her and kiss her. Equally astonishing, but fleeting, came the thought that she actually wouldn't mind a kiss from this man.

Her tongue flicked across her lips and she gave herself a mental shake, unable to turn away from his mesmerizing gaze. What could she be thinking? She had absolutely no business falling for a good-looking cowboy in the middle of nowhere. *Get a grip on yourself.*

Her heart quelled the voice of reason within her mind, as she stared into the cowboy's wide gray eyes. She broke his gaze and stared at her folded hands a second before she held them up in surrender.

"Okay, okay. I just don't know what came over me. I know you saw the parking space first. I guess I'm on bubba-overload. I apologize. Can I enter a plea of temporary insanity?" She placed her hands palms down on the table.

His gaze raked over her, one eyebrow elevated. "Well, well. I'm almost convinced there's true remorse here. Almost, but not quite. Would you like to explain to me what 'bubba-overload' is and what it has to do with me?"

"Listen, I apologized. Let's just drop it, okay?" Surprised at the petulant tone in her voice, she adjusted the dark green scarf that held the hair back from her face. With a toss of her head she sent auburn curls bouncing across her shoulders.

Will looked at her steadily, his voice polite but firm when

he spoke. "No, ma'am, we can't drop it. I think I deserve an explanation, especially after that 'bubba' remark. It sounded very much like an insult to me."

Aurora swiveled to face him as much as the limited space allowed. "Oh well, if you insist. You had on that western hat and were in a pickup truck. At a glance, you looked like the typical red-necked bubba. All you lacked was a big wad of tobacco bulging in your cheek."

She raised her hand and shook a finger at the man as if he were a naughty schoolboy. "Listen, I've had my fill and then some of you cowboys. You follow me, whistle at me, lean out a truck window to sing, shout or wave to me. Believe it or not, I do nothing either to initiate or encourage any of this behavior."

A skeptical smile appeared as he raised his eyebrows in silent question. The memory of the saucy kiss she'd blown to him in the parking lot popped into her mind and she blushed. She held up her hand to stop any comment he might make. "Oh, I know I was rude to you outside just now. Let me assure you, I'm not like that. In fact, it's truly a first."

She shook her head in wonder. "I don't know what came over me. As I said, I plead temporary insanity."

She looked down and pinched the fabric on the leg of the neatly creased blue denim jeans she wore. "Look at me. My jeans don't look as if they were painted on." She tugged at the hem of the hunter green knit top. "My shirt isn't too tight, it has three-quarter sleeves, and the neck isn't low or revealing."

Aurora moved her knees and elevated a foot to display canvas shoes below a dainty ankle. "I'm wearing Keds, not flashy pumps with stiletto heels. All in all, I think I'm dressed very sedately. Why should I attract any attention?"

The man slid a glance slowly up and down her and returned to her face. He gave her a slow, lazy smile that lit his eyes and brought a dimple to his cheek, but said nothing as he reached across her for the untouched glass of water at her right. His eyes returned to her as he sipped it.

Her own mouth opened as she watched his mouth against the rim of the glass. The tip of her pink tongue slid against her upper lip as the water slid into his mouth. She could almost feel his lips as they received the cool liquid. To hide her all too physical reaction, Aurora glared at him. In vain she tried to avoid thoughts of the meaning behind the look he sent or the effect of the deep dimple that appeared with his smile.

She forced herself to concentrate on her defense. "Um, I've never traveled through this part of Texas before. I just drive along, enjoying the scenery and minding my own business. I do nothing to call attention to myself. I even try to be a good sport about the immature behavior some guys display.

"I try to take it all in stride and just keep on schedule but"—Aurora slammed her hands against the top of the table—"this morning, two real bubbas almost ran me off the road passing me so they could whip their truck in front of mine. They were in a red Chevy truck exactly like the one you're driving." Aurora looked at him accusingly.

"Ma'am, most of the people in West Texas drive trucks, and an amazing number of them are red Chevys. You can't blame us all because of one reckless driver."

"Oh, that's not all. The passenger had the gall to moon me. Ooh, that made me so mad. I'm telling you, the more I thought about it, the angrier I became!" Aurora took a deep breath and looked at her hands.

"When I saw you sitting there in a truck like the one that

almost ran me off the road, I guess I just kind of lost it. Sorry about that." She leaned back and crossed her arms in front of her.

At this moment the waitress appeared with their food. Aurora stared in amazement as the waitress sat the burger, fries and soda in front of her and a duplicate of the order in front of the man beside her.

The waitress flashed what she probably thought of as her sexiest smile at the man as she said slowly, "Anything else today, Will?"

He seemed unaware of the flirtatiousness in her voice or the hopeful look in her eyes. "Not right now, Billie Ruth, thanks. Go ahead and leave the check and save yourself some time."

When the disappointed waitress left, Aurora gave Will an appraising look. How could he fail to notice the waitress's seductive tone? Had he any idea how attractive he is? This guy might be too good to be true. "How on earth did she know what to bring you? When did you give her your order?"

"When I came in," the man said as he leaned across her to get the salt and pepper. He paused and flashed her a truly breathtaking smile.

"I also told her you were picking up the check." Will saw the slight stiffening of the spine of the woman next to him and knew his remark ignited the sparks in those emerald eyes. He suppressed a chuckle. "Just kidding. But I'd like to prove all Texas truck drivers and cowboys aren't, uh, 'bubbas' like those you met this morning."

Aurora favored Will with a glare and concentrated on her food. Food always rated a high priority with her and the aroma of the meal in front of her increased her hunger. She immediately gave all her concentration to her delayed lunch.

Will watched in amused disbelief as Aurora took her hamburger apart to add ketchup. She spread the red glop evenly on the top half of the bun, and placed the tomato slice precisely in the middle of the meat patty. Then she carefully set the lettuce leaf on top. Next, she scraped off half the onions and part of the mustard from the bottom half of the bun. With a look of satisfaction, she reassembled the hamburger.

Catching his eyes on her actions, Aurora explained, "It's easier to redo a burger my way than to explain it when I order. No matter how detailed the explanation to the waitress, no one ever gets my hamburger right."

Will shook his head. "I had no idea a hamburger could be so complicated. I can hardly wait to see what you do with the french fries." This woman had to be the definitive control freak. Well, freak might be a bad choice of word, he mused. She was far too easy on the eyes for that designation.

Aurora took a large bite of her hamburger, obviously savoring the fresh-grilled flavor. After she swallowed, she looked at Will and asked, "So, what did you do to your leg?"

Will took a sip of his drink, then explained, "A few months ago we were moving some cattle from one range to another. This one big cow and her calf took off in the wrong direction and I rode around to turn her back."

An embarrassed look crept across his face. "I watched the cow instead of where I was going. My horse jumped a bush, but there was a big drop off on the other side. One minute I was sitting on my horse, the next minute the horse was lying on me. Worst of all, we'd fallen on a giant red ant mound. I broke my leg and I have to wear this thing for another month." He looked at his cast with disgust.

Aurora's normal good humor surfaced again. With wide eyes and a look of total innocence, she said, "Oh, my. That's too bad. I do hope the horse is okay."

"The horse is fine, thank you." Will flashed her a sardonic look. He should be angry at her teasing after she stole his parking spot, but her impish grin and sparkling green eyes were making him forget all about it.

He watched as she poured a neat pool of ketchup onto her plate and carefully dipped just the tip of each french fry into it. If he had a tape measure, he would bet that each dipped tip measured within a millimeter of the other.

The woman had to be crazy. Well, she seemed to be a nice crazy, and she was making him feel a little crazy himself. In fact, she made him feel a lot of things he hadn't felt in a very long time.

Will contemplated these new feelings with awe. After more than three years of widowhood, he felt—almost alive all of a sudden. And he kind of liked the feeling.

The flick of her tongue across her lips to catch an errant drop of ketchup made his dormant hormones stir. He shook his head slowly as if to clear his mind, still more than a little stunned by the feelings she aroused in him with just one look. Her eyes held an intelligence to match his own, and they suddenly lit up with an amused twinkle. Will had a feeling he was in for more teasing.

"I thought good guys wore white hats and bad guys wore black. Why is your hat gray? Does that mean you can't decide whether you're good or bad?"

Damn. She just wouldn't let up. This redhead really had his blood pressure rising. If she could read his thoughts, she would realize just how on the mark her question was. He adjusted his lanky frame on the booth seat.

"I'm not a bad guy, just a good guy who's a little worn

around the edges." Was that interest sparkling in her eyes? What was he going to do about it if it was? He felt way too out of practice for this kind of banter.

Aurora tried to look at him under her lashes so he wouldn't notice her interest. She could easily envision him as the cowboy hero in a western movie, calmly riding across the range into the sunset or galloping after the bad guys. His tall frame stretched under the table and his wide shoulders took up more than half the booth.

He was definitely handsome—and rugged. Aurora raised her eyes and flashed him a devilish smile.

"Will, huh? Not Billy Bob?"

He glared at her. Man, just when he had forgiven her, she started in on him again. This woman got under his skin in more ways than one. He put down his burger and wiped his hands first on a napkin and then on his jeans before he offered his right hand to her. In the confined space of the booth, this placed his hand almost in her lap.

"William Riley Harrison here."

Aurora dabbed at her hands with a napkin and took the hand he offered. "I'm Aurora Kathleen O'Shaughnessy. Please don't make any Irish jokes—believe me, I've heard them all. It really is my name, and I'm as American as you are."

As he grasped her hand and looked into her eyes, prickles moved along the back of her neck. Even her toes tingled. She felt as if she were gasping for breath. Could everyone in the restaurant hear her heart pounding against her ribs?

Get yourself under control, she chided. He's just a good-looking cowboy and you're a mature woman of twenty-eight, not a schoolgirl. It isn't as if you've never shaken hands with a man before.

Will chuckled. "Sounds like a lot of people have commented on that name. I don't think I've ever met anyone named Aurora."

Reluctantly, she removed her hand from his. "I was named after each grandmother. There are dozens of Kathleens in the family, but I'm the only one named after Grandmother Aurora. Grandmother Aurora was named after the town of Aurora. That's what Port Arthur, where I'm from, was once called."

"And what are you doing in Snyder? You must be new in town, since you were looking at a guidebook."

"Actually, I'm just passing through. I'm on my way to Colorado. I was heading for the Durango area."

Was that disappointment she saw on Will's face? But the look was only there a second before he countered, "Why Colorado?"

"A family friend there plans to sell her bookstore and has offered me first chance at it. I'll work with her a few weeks to be certain I really want to buy the store. She plans to retire in July."

Aurora took the last bite of her hamburger and swallowed. "What about you? Do you live in Snyder?"

"No, I have the Four H Ranch about thirty miles from here. Actually it's closer to Post than to Snyder."

Aurora twirled the straw in her drink as she gave him a quick appraisal. "Hmm, you look like a cowboy but you don't talk like one. Aren't you supposed to say things like *yup* and *dogie?*"

"Well, Gary Cooper I'm not," Will replied thoughtfully.

"Oh, yeah? He played a great cowboy—remember *High Noon?*" Without waiting for an answer, she continued, "Okay, so, you're not limited to *yup* and *nope* for conversation. What kind of cowboy are you then?"

"Hmm, well, a businessman/cowboy combination I

guess." He gave a shrug of his shoulder. "I think I'm just a typical West Texas rancher. I'm in town today as guest lecturer on local history to a class at the college."

Excitement bubbled up in Aurora. He neither looked nor acted typical to her. She might even be willing to make an unscheduled stop in Snyder if this handsome cowboy would volunteer to show her around the area personally.

"Oh, really? My father is a history professor and I'm a devoted history buff myself. Maybe you could make a few suggestions for a half day's tour of the town."

As he reached for her guidebook across the table, Aurora saw the gold band on the third finger of his left hand. The depth of disappointment she felt surprised her as her eyes scanned his deeply tanned face. Yes, Will Harrison was definitely very handsome in a rugged way, and intelligent too. What a terrific combination. Just as well he was taken, because she certainly didn't need to complicate her life.

Silent while he glanced at the listings for the area, Will returned to the Snyder portion of the guidebook. When he half-turned and leaned toward her, it seemed as if he folded her into his body while he pointed to the page.

"You should definitely see the museum at the college— that's the Scurry County Museum at Western Texas College. Oh, and don't miss the statue of the white buffalo on the courthouse square."

He glanced at his watch. "I have an appointment in a little while to get this cast changed. If you plan to be around later, I'd like to show you around some. There are quite a few interesting sites in Scurry and Garza Counties that aren't listed."

She fumed. And what would he tell his wife, the handsome rat? The nerve of this man—he probably even had children as well as a wife.

Her answer was cool. "Thanks, but on second thought I'll probably just spend a couple of hours here and head on toward Lubbock. Might even make Amarillo by tonight."

Aurora wiped her lips and hands with a fresh napkin from the dispenser on the table. She reached for the check but a large hand covered hers as Will slid the check away with his other hand. An electric connection traveled from her hand and spread throughout her body.

So this is what you've come to, now you're turned on by a married man. Have you gone crazy? She scolded herself silently. She quickly withdrew her hand and slipped the strap of her handbag onto her shoulder.

"I told you I was kidding about making you pay the check," Will said. "After all, you're a guest in the area." He flashed his devastating smile again. "I guess I'd also better not ask you to make good on that kiss you blew me outside."

"Thank you." Aurora felt her annoyingly fair skin go red again as she chewed on her bottom lip. She became distant once more. "Since you're being so gracious, I guess I'll have to let you take care of the check." Sure, let the double-dealing cheat get stuck picking up the tab for her meal. Served him right.

"Well, thanks again for the food and sightseeing tips. It's difficult for you to get up, so I'll just use an unconventional exit route." Aurora stood on the seat and stepped over the back of the booth onto the now empty seat of the booth behind them. Then she jumped down onto the floor and escaped, ignoring the stares of the staff and the other diners.

Will sat a few minutes longer, puzzled by Aurora's sudden change in attitude and hasty exit. While they ate they had talked pleasantly and he'd enjoyed her company, once his initial anger had subsided. He felt certain he'd seen an interested sparkle in her eyes. He knew he was out of practice, but that flirtatious twinkle and her inviting smile were unmistakable. Out of practice he might be; dead, he was not.

Why had her manner changed so suddenly? Had he completely misread her interest? No, something had happened or been said about the time they finished eating. He reviewed their conversation in his mind, but found nothing he did or said that could have caused the sudden chilliness in her attitude.

Will reached for the crutches and, in doing so, looked down at his own hand. The wedding ring—that must be it! He grabbed the crutches angrily and cursed to himself. His discussion with his daughter earlier that morning flashed through his mind. Damn! That wedding ring scared Aurora off. Kelly had been right.

For the first time since the death of his wife, he wanted to spend time with a woman. Now that he met a woman who actually interested him, not only was she just passing through town but she probably thought that he was a philandering married man.

No wonder her attitude had changed. Cursing to himself again, he ran his fingers through his already tousled hair before he jammed his hat onto his head.

He restrained the impulse to rush to the college museum, find her and explain. His leg hurt like hell and reminded him of his appointment at Nick Harris's orthopedic clinic. Nick was his friend as well as his doctor. Maybe he could see him quickly, Will thought—and then he could catch Aurora at the museum before she left town.

But Nick and his staff conspired to waste most of his afternoon fussing over his leg. Finally, the doctor changed the cast to a slightly shorter, lighter one and released him.

Will raced to the museum parking lot to search for Aurora's blue Mustang. No luck. It was nowhere in sight.

After a pass by the courthouse, still with no sight of Aurora or her car, Will gave up and started home. All day long, thunderclouds had gathered overhead. Now the sky was nearly black, with ominous rumbles and brilliant flashes of lightning. Rain fell in giant drops, slowly at first but rapidly increased in intensity. The terrible weather definitely matched Will's mood.

Chapter Two

After a tour of the college museum, Aurora decided to visit the college library to research the history of the area. She became so engrossed that she lost track of the time. Then the flickering library lights and loud rumbles of thunder reminded her she needed to be on her way.

With regret Aurora thought of the handsome cowboy she'd met in the restaurant. Until she'd seen his wedding band, she'd thought of him as someone nice who seemed to share many of her interests. In addition, he was obviously intelligent. It would've been great to have someone like him—someone unmarried—as a guide of the area. She sighed. It would be great to have someone like him for anything.

She would just have to remember to stick to her plans. Business and independence first, then romance—on her terms. Later, after her business was firmly established, would come marriage and a family. Follow the schedule, she reminded herself once more.

Heavy rainfall made progress on U.S. Highway 84 very slow. Several vehicles pulled to the side of the road to wait out the downpour, but Aurora pressed onward. The turmoil of the day and the future decisions she faced left her weary from fatigue. All her thoughts centered on a hot shower in a comfortable motel in Post.

She drove into the fast-moving water before she realized she had crossed not just a low spot in the highway, but the edge of some overflowing watercourse that rushed madly across the asphalt. She tried to reverse the car, but the low-slung Mustang stalled. Aurora tried to remain calm, but that was a lost cause. The water around the car was rising rapidly.

She had to salvage what she could and get to higher ground—pronto. Aurora slipped the strap of her handbag over her head and pulled the scarf from her hair. She quickly tied one end to her wrist and the other to the halogen torch from her dashboard compartment.

She had to save her briefcase above all. It contained her laptop computer and financial records. She might manage with one suitcase and her briefcase but everything else would have to be abandoned. With great difficulty, she struggled to open the door against the pressure of the rising water. But cold, muddy water rushed into the car as she struggled to get out.

Some days, Will Harrison's very soul reverberated with anger directed toward every aspect of his life. His heart throbbed with anger at the cancer that had robbed him of his sweet wife Nancy three years earlier. Every breath sent blood pulsing to his brain in anger toward the cow he chased when his horse fell on him, causing him months of pain and inconvenience. The very center of his being filled with hatred against the drought that baked his land dry and hard as stone and kept the grassland from growing last summer. He knew it was useless but he still raged against the deluge which now flooded his ranch and caused his lights and phone to fail. Many of his cattle were probably stranded or drowned.

Finally, he felt angry with that woman—Aurora. His sense of logic told him it was irrational to be angry with a beautiful woman he'd met only once. Yet his emotions said otherwise—especially in his current mood. He accepted the responsibility for Aurora's mistaken impression of him, but the anger remained.

He flexed his left hand several times and looked at the finger where his wedding ring had been for so many years. What would Nancy think of his recent behavior? They had intended the vows to last forever—and he had never taken off the ring she'd given him since the day they were married.

Even thoughts of another woman made him feel as unfaithful as Aurora probably labeled him. Would he ever overcome this feeling? Will doubted anyone could ever take Nancy's place. He struck the window frame with the side of his fist, then leaned his forehead against the cool glass. If only these memories of Nancy hurt less.

Though he might never see Aurora again, he had found her intriguing and very much wanted to be near her again. More than that, he felt a kinship with her and found her quick wit stimulating. That surprised him.

Her body stimulated him in a different way, which also surprised him. She resurrected feelings he thought long dead. He saw her in his mind as clearly as if she stood in front of him: thick auburn curls falling over her shoulders and green eyes flashing. Her sassy smile had beguiled him, and he'd been more than tempted to kiss those rosy lips.

Will ran his fingers through his hair. Why even think about her? All that talk with Kelly and Lily this morning had started it. He just got caught off guard, that's all.

Even as the thought popped into his mind, he knew he was lying to himself. There seemed something special about Aurora. At least, for a little while, she made him feel alive again. For a brief time today he had forgotten to mourn.

Will gazed once more through the window in front of

him and cursed the weather. At least his daughter was high and dry, over at her grandmother's house for a sleepover. He'd rather not worry about her any more than he already did.

Watching the much-needed rain fall far too rapidly to soak into the hard-packed earth, he frowned. With his sleeve, he rubbed at the window, unsure of what he saw. Was there a light moving on the railroad tracks?

He watched closely as the beam flickered on the wet rails, and watched a few seconds more. Someone was walking along the tracks.

Who would be out in this storm? Only someone stranded by rising water would seek the high ground of the railroad bed.

Will saw the light stop briefly before it streaked down the bank of the road bed and sank beneath the water. Perhaps the mysterious person dropped the light—or was he imagining things?

No. He saw the light resurface and shine from the largest of the cottonwood trees by the creek. Will watched with fascination until he realized that whoever was walking on the rails probably had fallen into the water, climbed into the tree, and was still clutching the flashlight.

Will grabbed his crutches firmly and moved rapidly across the room. It wasn't going to be easy, but he had to help. Come hell or high water.

Aurora clung to the trunk of the large cottonwood tree in which she perched. Her head and left side ached horribly from her collision with the tree after her fall into the flood water, and she was seeing stars.

Now she thought she saw the headlights of a car or truck moving toward the railroad bed. Perhaps a concussion could do that, could make a person see all kinds of strange lights. Her eyes blinked and she tried to focus. A wave of nausea diverted her attention, and she retched into the muddy water beneath her.

Suddenly, a light beamed her way from the tracks and she heard a man's voice call over the sound of the storm. She directed the beam of her own torch in his direction. The light revealed a man on crutches. His face was blurred in rain and shadow, but she thought instantly of the man she'd met earlier in the day. This must be that cheating cowboy, Will Harrison. After all, how many men on crutches could live in the middle of nowhere?

Giant bolts of lightning reached across the night sky to spread an eerie illumination. Will tied one end of the rope to the railroad track. He coiled the remainder of the rope in his hands and yelled at her to grab the loop he threw. Time after time, the rope hit the tree limbs or fell beyond her grasp.

At last Aurora caught it and almost fell from the tree in the process. Dangling precariously, she slid the rope over her head and secured it under her arms.

The man knelt on one knee with the other leg stuck out at an angle. Suddenly, her body jerked as the rope went taut and pain of a new kind shot through her back and ribs. She struggled, powerless against the raging torrent as her cold and stiffened muscles refused to cooperate.

In agony, she finally felt the road bed beneath her feet as he pulled her closer. She grabbed the hand the kneeling man offered, and he pulled the rope with one hand as he used the other to hoist her near him. The rain pelted fiercely, and the night was as black as ink between flashes of lightning.

Will stared in disbelief at the face before him. "Aurora?

What in the hell are you doing here?"

"Well, I didn't just decide to go for a swim," she yelled back at him while rain streamed down her face and plastered her hair to her head.

The trek to the truck and ride to Will's home was a blur. For once in her life Aurora simply followed directions without question. As the flashes of lightning revealed the shapes of outbuildings, she gave thanks. Soon she would be in a house. Soon she would be warm and dry.

"The electricity's off and I haven't started the emergency generator yet. Bring your torch. I'll get the luggage later. First, we need to get you warm and dry."

Aurora followed him into the house, oblivious to the trail of mud and water she left with every step. Just through a laundry room, Will led her to a large bathroom.

"Get your clothes off and get into the shower. I'll start the generator so the electric pump on the well can run. Only the water pump and appliances are hooked up to the generator. There still won't be any light."

Will pulled a couple of towels out of the linen closet. "My robe is hanging on the door here. Looks like your torch batteries are almost gone. When I get the generator going, I'll get another lantern."

He gave her an appraising look and a frown creased his forehead. She still looked stunned. Her pupils were much too dilated. "Will you be all right here while I go start the generator?"

Aurora gave him a dazed stare. "Why, yes, thank you. I'll be just fine," she said primly as if theirs were the most normal of circumstances.

That worried him, but he had to leave her a few minutes. "Don't lock the bathroom door. If you fall or pass out, I don't want to have to pick the lock."

Aurora sank to the floor. She knew she should get up and do something, something he told her. What had he said? She just couldn't remember. As if in a trance, she removed the canvas shoes and peeled off her socks. The torch bounced against her body as she raised her hand to her head. She felt the back of her head and discovered a huge lump where her head had hit the tree. When she looked at her hand, there was blood. No wonder her head hurt so abominably. No wonder she couldn't think.

When Will returned with a battery-powered lantern, he found the bathroom door open and Aurora seated on the floor. She worked to untie the scarf that bound the torch to her hand. He bent to help her, and used his pocket knife to cut the cloth. The scarf had chafed her wrist badly but had probably saved her life by preventing the loss of the torch. Its flickering beam had alerted Will to her plight and guided him to her rescue.

Aurora offered no protest when Will pulled her to her feet and undressed her as if she were a small child. She winced and moaned when he pulled her knit top off over her head, but made no other comments. When Will saw her back, he gasped as he unfastened her bra. Even in the dim light her injuries shocked him.

"My God! You've really messed up your back. You might have broken ribs."

"I . . . I don't know," Aurora said weakly. "It's this lump on my head that hurts most." She touched the spot once more and tried to remember the details of her accident.

Feeling slowly returned to her numbed limbs. Her senses, too, slowly awakened. She could smell him again—she thought she would never forget that smell, the smell which her tired brain now identified with safety. The fragrance of damp hair and healthy maleness replaced the earlier aftershave. Alive and safe now, memories whirled in her head.

"Huge. It was huge." She struggled to make sense of her jumbled thoughts. "I saw a huge water moccasin—biggest snake I've ever seen 'cept in a zoo. I only wanted to sit on my suitcase and rest a bit. I was so tired—felt like I walked hours and hours in that awful rain."

She pressed her forehead with her hand. Memories of her trek through the storm, the difficulty pushing and dragging her cases, and of the frightening snake still were very real. "As I put the cases down that horrid thing crawled right at me. I think I jumped back from it and slipped." She shuddered. "I tried to swim, but the current was too strong and slammed me into that big tree."

Will felt a weakness in his stomach as he thought of what might have happened when she'd fallen into the flood waters. His voice was quiet. "That tree saved your life. You couldn't have managed to swim in the flooded creek."

He scanned the flashlight over her back. "I'm going to touch your ribs as gently as I can and see if I can feel a break." Will probed softly at her rib cage and shoulder. "I've seen guys in the rodeo look better than this after being stomped by a bull."

Aurora winced but he continued. When he held her shoulder while he rotated her arm, she almost passed out from the pain.

Will shook his head. She must have endured tremendous pain as she struggled through the storm. Why had she dragged that damn suitcase and briefcase? As harebrained as it seemed, she had pluck, he would give her that.

"If there's a fracture, I don't think I'd be able to feel it, but there doesn't seem to be a break and your shoulder's not dislocated. Did you throw up blood?"

Aurora tried to concentrate. It was as if a delay existed from the time she heard sounds until her brain could process what she heard and respond. "I don't know . . . I don't taste blood, just muddy water."

"Can you take a shower by yourself?"

Aurora nodded her head and immediately regretted the action. "I need to lie down." She grabbed Will's arm with one hand and put her other hand to her forehead while the floor spun around.

"I know you do, but we have to get you cleaned up first. Floodwater is septic even in the wide-open spaces around here, so we need to get these cuts washed out and treated with antibiotic cream. It'll take a while for the water heater to get hot, but the water that's in the tank now is probably still warm enough for a quick shower if you don't mix cold with it." Will talked as he worked at the zipper of her jeans.

Aurora placed her hands over his and frowned. Where were the other people who lived in this big house? Even with her trouble concentrating, she remembered the wedding ring he wore at lunch. "You shouldn't be doing this. Can't your wife help me?"

Will's voice came sharp and terse. "No, I'm the only one here. My wife died three years ago. You'll just have to put up with me for the time being."

As quickly as possible, Will stripped her jeans down and helped her step out of them. Aurora's knees looked like hamburger and scratches decorated her entire body.

His eyes met hers and he took a deep breath. One more big hurdle, he thought. "Brace yourself and pretend I'm your grandmother," he said, and then quickly jerked down the panties which were her only remaining clothing. He turned on the shower and checked the water temperature before he helped her in.

"You'll have to hurry before all the warm water's gone." As Aurora stood under the stream, Will grabbed some shampoo from the ledge of the shower and poured a little onto her hair. "Work that into your hair and rinse it out. Try to clean the area of the lump especially well."

Will took a bar of soap and lathered his hand. With quick but gentle movements, he ran his lathered hand over the injured portion of her back, knees and legs. The dim light in the bathroom hid the red flush creeping over him as he touched her satiny skin.

He stepped away from her just long enough to rummage in the bathroom cabinet and locate the hydrogen peroxide.

"Rinse your mouth out with peroxide, and that'll have to do for now. If you're through with your hair, come on out and I'll help you dry off."

As Aurora stepped from the shower to the wet tile of the bathroom floor, she slipped and grabbed for his arm. Before he realized he had moved, his arms were at her waist, steadying her against his chest. "Lord, give me strength," he muttered under his breath.

Will tried not to look at her body, not to look at her as a man looks at a woman, but he couldn't help himself. Her legs were long and slim, her waist small below ample breasts. If it were not for the bruises and cuts, her fair skin would be flawless. Certain he viewed the most beautiful woman he'd ever met, heat coursed through his body to pool in his loins.

The minute that thought appeared, he once again felt disloyal to Nancy. He cursed to himself. In a part of his mind, he remained married, regardless of the three years since Nancy's death or the absence of his wedding ring.

After Aurora's one inquiry about his wife, she gave in to his ministrations. Will gently dabbed the towel over her body while Aurora braced herself with her right hand on his shoulder. He helped her into his robe of heavy toweling fabric. The warm, dry robe felt wonderfully soft against her skin and she clutched it around her.

"This way, Aurora, just follow me." Will managed to use the crutches while juggling the battery-powered lantern to guide Aurora through the house.

He yanked down the covers of the bed to make a place for her. "Wait on the bed." The light of an old-fashioned kerosene lamp on the bedside table gave the room a soft glow. "I'll get the antibiotic cream and some of your clothes."

Aurora eased her body onto the bed, her right side facing the wall, and curled into a ball. She hurt everywhere and wanted nothing as much as to sleep for days. It felt so good to be out of the rain and lying on a real bed at last. She heard Will returning but could not force herself to move.

"Everything in the suitcase is damp or wet. You'll have to settle for something of mine." He hobbled over to a chest across the room and pulled a pair of pajamas out of a drawer.

"Come on, sit up," Will instructed as he took Aurora's right hand and tugged gently.

Aurora responded, "I'm fine like this. I just want to sleep."

Will sorted through the first aid supplies. "No, don't conk out on me yet. Come on, sit up."

She tried to push his hands away. "I have to sleep."

He repeated, "Not yet. We have to treat those scrapes. We'll start with your head and work down," Will said as he applied peroxide to a ball of cotton. He gently cleaned and applied antibiotic cream to each wound before he helped her into his pajama top.

"Oh. This feels nice. Silk satin, isn't it?" Aurora still sounded dazed as she looked down at the green top she wore while Will rolled up the sleeves to fit her arms. The man's extra-tall sized top covered her to mid-thigh, almost like a short nightgown.

"Yes, my Aunt Rose gave these pajamas to me for Christmas. She knows I never wear pajamas but she hopes to civilize me someday."

Together they managed to get rid of the robe and settle her into bed. She still felt no embarrassment from him seeing her body. That was enough proof for her that she was definitely suffering from shock. In fact, it was the only possible explanation.

Here they were, two people cut off from the rest of the world. She should be wary of the isolation with a man she'd met only once before. Instead, she felt secure, safe from the storm and the cares of the world outside the house that now served as her refuge. The protected feeling surprised her.

A fresh wave of nausea swept through her but there was nothing left in her stomach. When the heaving ceased, she snuggled her face into the pillow, intent on sleep.

Will touched her shoulder gently. "Listen, you can't go to sleep now. Come on, sit up again so you can stay awake a little longer. That's quite a bump on your head and you might have a concussion. Try to stay awake while I get one more thing."

She heard him leave the room but lost all track of time while she floated in the cocoon of warmth that engulfed her. He returned with a loud din. A bucket dangled from his hand and clattered against the crutch with each step. After he set the bucket on the floor, he delved into it to retrieve a cup and a thermos. Waves of steam issued from the open mouth of the thermos when he poured hot tea into the cup.

"Drink this to help counteract the shock"—he reached into the bucket and brought out some crackers—"and these crackers might help the nausea."

The tea laced with honey tasted far too sweet. Heat from the cup felt good to her icy hands, though. She sipped from the cup and held the warm tea in her mouth before letting it slide down her throat to soothe her quaking stomach.

When she seemed somewhat more comfortable, Will picked up the cellular phone from his bedside table. He dialed his friend Nick's home number and felt a surge of relief when Nick answered. Will explained what had happened to Aurora and Nick recommended what treatment he could, considering their isolated circumstances. Then Will made his way to the other side of the bed. Weariness showed in the slump of his body as he sighed and unfastened the buttons of his shirt.

Aurora's eyes grew wide and she gasped before her temper flared. "What do you think you're doing?"

He took a deep breath before answering. "Look, Nick said I have to watch you, especially through tonight, to make certain there are no potentially serious complications. He thinks you probably do have a concussion."

Aurora studied him woozily. "So?"

"This is a king-sized bed, and I'm far too tired to sit up the rest of the night. I have to get this leg elevated and get some rest, and it has to be soon. You just keep pretending I'm your grandmother, and I'll lie right here and watch over you while you sleep."

Aurora lay facing him, suddenly too weary to move. Her brief spate of temper ebbed and with it any remaining strength. Slowly, reason reappeared and she evaluated her position and Will's.

Maneuvering along the railroad track to rescue her must

have been torture for him. Still, he continued to help her here at the house when he had to be badly in need of rest himself. She must seem a bad-tempered ingrate.

"Thank you for rescuing me . . . and for taking care of me. I don't think I could have held onto that tree much longer. There's no doubt in my mind that you saved my life tonight."

Will sat on the side of the bed and looked over at her briefly, then ran his hand through his hair. "You had one hell of a day, didn't you?" He removed the boot and sock from his right foot and the remains of the torn plastic trash bag still taped to the cast on his left leg.

Aurora couldn't help but appreciate his muscular body as he stood in the soft lantern light. Without his shirt, his shoulders seemed even wider and his chest broader. Muscles rippled as he ripped most of the left leg from the pajama bottom to accommodate his cast. Startled, she gasped again when he unzipped his jeans and lowered them. Aurora felt her face grow warm with a blush. She closed her eyes as she burrowed her head into her pillow.

"I wondered how long your observation would last," he said quietly, and chuckled. She pretended not to hear him, embarrassed to be caught staring.

After he lowered the wick on the lantern and lay down, Will said, "I hope I can stay awake. If you need anything during the night and I've fallen asleep, just reach out and shake me gently to wake me."

"All right, but I think I'll be fine if I can just sleep."

"Goodnight, Aurora."

A glimmer of humor surfaced in Aurora's tired mind. "Goodnight, grandmother." She could not resist adding, "What long legs you have."

Will closed his eyes and smiled. "Thanks."

Chapter Three

Once again Aurora felt herself falling into the raging flood. Rolling water sucked downward and downward, her lungs crying for air and about to burst. She struggled for the surface, fighting against the force of the current and the debris that slammed into her.

Deeper and deeper she sank in the swirling, muddy water, lungs desperate for air, as she choked, drowning . . . Suddenly, she awakened with a start.

Will said softly, "Having a nightmare?"

"Yes. Sorry if I disturbed you. I'll try to lie very still. I keep reliving my fall into the water. I try to swim, but I feel myself sinking and drowning," Aurora answered without moving or opening her eyes.

Her eyes flew open as she felt the bed move. "What are you doing?"

"Aw, surely you don't think I'm making a pass at you in your condition? I'm scooting a little closer so you can give me your hand. Maybe if you hold my hand while you go to sleep, it'll keep you from having nightmares."

"Oh." Aurora reached for his strong hand and held it as naturally as if she did so every night. Soon she drifted to sleep. This time no nightmares plagued her rest.

It was the pain in her back and shoulder which caused her to awaken hours later. The lantern still burned very low. Will's closed eyes and soft breathing gave no clues to whether he slept or merely rested.

From far away came the low call of a train whistle. She

had lost all sense of time, but she knew it had been hours since Will rescued her. She would have waited hours in that tree for this train, *if* she could've managed to attract the engineer's attention with her halogen torch and *if* the torch batteries hadn't gone dead by then.

Thoughts of her fate if Will had not come sent chills down her spine. She could not have held on to that tree, and the raging torrent would have claimed her as it had in her nightmare. Aurora trembled uncontrollably.

A strong arm slipped around her waist. Will patted her gently as he slid closer to her. "It's all right, Aurora. It's all right. You're safe here now with me," he said, his voice soft and gentle. "Don't think about the flood or the storm anymore. Think about something pleasant and go back to sleep."

Aurora felt his breath near her hair. As she turned her face to rest against his shoulder, her hand slid to his chest. Will's arms tightened and he softly kissed her hair.

"Everything will work out, you'll see."

Nestled there, she forgot the vows she made to herself, her neatly planned schedule for her life. Forgotten were her plans to avoid dependence on any man. This feeling of protection and security soothed her battered body and bruised soul. She nestled against his shoulder and drifted gratefully back to sleep, warm and shielded against the storm which still raged outside.

Gray light poured through the window between parted draperies and raised blinds when Aurora awakened. As she tried organizing her thoughts about her experiences of the previous day, she looked about the room in which she lay. The decor was distinctively masculine, but very attractive.

On one of the walls and on most pieces of the furniture

were photographs of a little girl at various ages. Prominent in the arrangement of photographs on the wall hung a wedding photograph of a younger Will. How proud and carefree he looked beside his bride. Hanging nearby, another photograph showed an older Will, his wife, and the little girl.

Aurora tried to focus on the face of the petite, brown-haired woman with brown eyes. She looked kind, with a sweet smile on a face very much like that of the little girl.

Nature called, and Aurora could lie there no longer. She wanted her handbag and luggage. First she would find the bathroom, then search for her belongings and her host.

When she found him, he stood at the kitchen range in front of a skillet of sizzling ham slices. Will wore fresh jeans and a red plaid shirt. He'd shaved, and his hair was brushed but still wet. A newscaster announced details of the flood through the portable radio on the counter.

The kitchen was a large airy room with windows across the wall of the breakfast nook and a door opening onto a patio beside the windows. There, spread out to dry on the dark oak table in the breakfast nook, were the contents of Aurora's handbag. Nearby, her briefcase had been opened to air, and she noticed the deep scars and scrapes on the outside. Will must have towed it behind him to the truck. From the direction of the garage, she heard the steady hum of a machine that probably was the emergency generator.

A frown furrowed his brow when he saw her. "Hey, you shouldn't be up. You're supposed to rest until Doctor Nick can check you over." He let his gaze run over her, and a smile replaced the frown. "You're looking much perkier than I would have expected, though."

"What are you doing?" she asked testily, ignoring his remarks as she stood framed in the doorway. She tugged at the hem of the pajama top and walked into the room.

Will knew he stared. How could this woman with a mass of tangled auburn hair and skinned knees, clad only in his oversized pajama top, be so attractive? She seemed unaware of just how sexy she looked. The pajama top covered only the first few inches of her thighs and left her long shapely legs bare. Even in her disheveled state she was beautiful. His pulse raced at the sight of her.

"I'm cooking breakfast." When he noticed her attention focused on the contents of her handbag, he explained, "I tried to get the mud off the things from your handbag and lay them out to dry. They aren't in very good shape, I'm afraid, and some are probably ruined."

He nodded toward the briefcase. "The briefcase seems to have made out fine. The lid sealed tight and no water got inside. Sorry about the scrapes on the outside of the cases. The stuff in the suitcase was mostly just damp, but everything smells kind of strange."

He turned back to the range, grabbed the skillet, and turned off the flame. "How do you feel?"

Embarrassed, she thought, for her earlier assumption that he had rifled through her things to satisfy his curiosity. Aloud she said, "Like a hundred-year-old woman who's been mugged. I'm in search of a hairbrush, toothpaste, and toothbrush." She inspected the articles on the table.

Will nodded toward another door. "Your suitcase is in there. It's five minutes until breakfast is ready, so hurry or your breakfast will be cold."

Aurora went in the direction he indicated. Hurry? How could she hurry on muscles so stiff she could only wobble? The unusual and slightly lopsided hairdo which resulted from her head injury matched the desolate look on her face when she returned to the kitchen.

"How about some ham and eggs?"

"Looks delicious. I didn't think I could eat anything until I saw the food." Aurora looked for a clean spot on the cluttered table.

"Let's sit at the breakfast island if you feel well enough. I seem to have made a mess of the table."

She eased her battered body gently onto a bar stool. With a tug, she yanked the pajama top down to cover as much of her legs as possible and realized just how much of her body the pajama top exposed. She wished she had remembered to grab that robe of Will's.

Will pretended not to notice her adjustments to her attire as he set two plates down on the counter top and reached into a drawer for cutlery. In fact, though, he noticed every movement she made, every inadvertent exposure of satiny skin. How was he supposed to control himself with her looking like that?

"I made more of the sweetened tea you had last night. I've always heard tea's best for nausea. I have instant coffee, though, if you'd rather have that."

"This looks perfect." Aurora, hurting and hungry, cared nothing about details. "Let's eat."

"Hmm, sounds like you're really hungry. Did you have any dinner yesterday?" Will used his crutches to hobble to a stool at the end of the breakfast bar.

"The last time I ate was with you in Snyder . . . except for the tea and crackers you gave me last night." Aurora looked around the room to get her bearings. "That seems like a long time ago."

"Doesn't it though? You sure had an A-1 example of a bad day yesterday, didn't you?"

Will watched in fascination as she ate, certain she sliced each bite of ham into precisely the same size and shape. As she leaned toward the bar to eat, the neck of the oversized pajama top fell forward to reveal her perfect breasts.

His pulse beat faster and he stared at her, mesmerized. She sat with each of her legs hooked around a leg of the bar stool, leaving her thighs parted slightly. He drank the glow of her perfect skin, her well-shaped face, ample breasts, and long shapely legs. The knee of one of her legs almost touched his own. If he reached out . . .

My God, what on earth am I thinking? This woman is a guest in my home, someone who needs my care and protection. How can I even think of taking advantage of her? And why is it this one woman causes my hormones to rage when other women don't even interest me?

Will ran his fingers through his hair and hoped Aurora picked up nothing of his lecherous feelings. This was going to be a very long day.

Aurora's voice brought Will back to consciousness. "May I use your cellular phone if the phone lines are still out? I call my family at prearranged times, you see, and I was supposed to check in with them last night."

"Sure. We also need to alert the sheriff in case someone sees your abandoned car and starts a search for you. I talked with my family in Lubbock last night, so apparently only the rural phone lines are out."

Aurora sighed heavily.

"My cell phone was one of the first casualties of last night's storm. I suppose my car is a goner, too."

"Well, if it ever turns up, it might be a total loss. It's probably mired in several feet of sandy mud right now. With any luck it'll run aground before it reaches the Brazos River."

"Well, it's insured. But it'll take several days to put in for the loss and get my car replaced." Already, she was organizing the reporting process in her mind.

"Try weeks."

"Weeks? Oh, my." Aurora's expression of surprise turned pensive. "Hmm, in that case, I'd better find a temporary job that doesn't require a car," she said as if to herself.

She caught his questioning look. "I'm not broke or anything, but I'm conserving my cash until I see how much I need to relocate to Durango and buy that bookstore I told you about."

She tapped her nails on the countertop. "Of course, it would probably be best to move on at least as far as Lubbock, but there's still the chance that my car might be found."

"What sort of work do you do?"

"Well, my degree is in marketing, and I just left a job with a firm in Houston where I was a junior partner. Carter, James and Carter—maybe you've heard of them. When I was in school, though, I worked as a secretary, receptionist, file clerk, dormitory assistant, and even did a stint for an accounting firm at income tax time."

Will looked incredulous. "You left a junior partnership with Carter, James and Carter to buy a bookstore in Durango?" What could have caused this woman to make such a drastic change in her life? Even he had heard of the firm she left, and to be a junior partner there was quite an achievement. Before he knew it the question spilled forth. "I guess this big career move means you're not currently, um, what do they say . . . now with a significant other?"

Aurora looked down at her hands to hide the pain that question revived. "Well, I was engaged, but right now he's getting married to someone else. He actually congratulated me on my career change the last time I saw him. That was just before Christmas."

She raised her head, slightly embarrassed. "Oh, my. I

haven't spoken of Russell to anyone in four months. I didn't intend to mention that part of my life ever again."

Will grabbed her plate, stacked it on top of his, and went over to the kitchen sink, edging along the kitchen counter. "Your secret's safe with me. I'm not likely to tell anyone."

Will wondered what kind of jerk the guy who'd dumped her must be, but it didn't seem like the kind of thing he could ask her. At least not right now.

Aurora yawned, and looked around the kitchen.

"Okay. I'd better call my folks. I wish my head would stop aching." She looked over to the things spread out across the kitchen table. "Do you remember seeing any aspirin in all this stuff?"

"No, but I left some on the bedside table last night. Nick said you should spend the day resting to give your body time to recover. If you'll get back in bed after you take the aspirin, you'll find the phone on the table near my side of the bed."

Aurora blushed slightly at his phrasing. It sounded as if they always shared a bed. She found it a very pleasant thought, and the blush deepened. Remember your resolve, girl, she thought as she watched Will lean against the kitchen counter.

Okay, she admitted, he really makes your pulse race. In her mind she could still feel the touch of his hands as he helped her bathe. As a person who valued both privacy and independence, she found it hard to believe she still felt no embarrassment that he had seen her naked.

Once again she relived the warmth of his arm around her and the gentle touch of his lips as he kissed her hair. How could such simple gestures bring such security?

She longed for him to repeat those gestures, to feel his arm around her once more. What would happen if she stood in front of him and leaned against that expansive chest? Would he encircle her with his arms, or think she had gone crazy?

Aloud, she only asked, "I suppose we're trapped by the water?"

"I'm afraid so. According to the radio, over ten inches of rain fell last night and we'll probably get more today. It's a record amount of rain in that time span, or so the announcer said. Certainly I can't remember water this high before, so I guess he's right."

"I believe that. For a while last night I thought I must have missed the ark." When she saw the look on his face, her smile changed to concern. "Oh, Will, I'm so sorry. Here I worry about my car and a few clothes and things. You must be worried sick about your ranch and your stock."

His brow furrowed in worry. "Yes, and this damn cast won't help me get around to see about them."

"How long will we be cut off by the flood?"

"Unless we get another downpour, the roads will probably be open by late today—tomorrow for sure. I'll check with the sheriff when I call him about your car. In the meantime, you need to rest. Want another ice pack?"

The pounding in her head increased in intensity with every minute she stayed upright. "No, I don't want the ice pack. I guess you're right about the rest, though. I really do need to lie down now."

As Aurora slid off the bar stool, the pull of the vinyl cushion against her bare skin once again reminded her that she still wore only Will's pajama top. What was happening to her? She wasn't acting like herself at all. It must be the concussion.

She walked as sedately as possible back to the bedroom. With a big sigh, she crawled into bed and sank back onto the pillows.

Chapter Four

Aurora's parents were just as upset as she had feared, even though she glossed over the loss of her car and totally omitted her trip along the railroad tracks and fall into the floodwater. When she hung up, she looked up to find Will giving her an assessing gaze.

"What?" she asked, innocently enough.

"You weren't exactly honest with your parents, Aurora."

"Yes, I was. Unless you mean lies by omission." Aurora crossed her arms across her chest, then raised her chin and said primly, "It would be counterproductive to give too many details and worry them when there's nothing to be gained by it."

That sounded far more severe than she intended, so she added more. "They're somewhat overprotective since I got unengaged last December. They think I'm crazy to quit my job and put everything on hold while I check out this bookstore, even though the owner is their friend."

"And are you?"

"What? Crazy? No, quite the opposite." Her arms relaxed. She paused to remember the person she had been. Working endless hours for Carter, James and Carter had left virtually no time for herself. "Once I made the decision to leave Houston, I vowed to simplify my life. I decided on my goals and set up a carefully planned schedule to achieve them."

Aurora twisted the sheet with her fingers and raised her eyes to Will. She wished he weren't so close, that his eyes weren't quite such an attractive shade of gray or his mouth so inviting. She tried to focus on her explanation.

"Many people find city life exciting, but I really didn't like Houston."

In light of her recent travels it seemed absurd that she had actually lived in Houston, commuting downtown in stifling humidity to fight her way through hordes of other commuters to reach her office. Now the mere thought of facing that every day appalled her. She shook her head slowly in wonder at the change in her attitude over the past few months—a change that still surprised her.

"Well, after Russell broke our engagement, I reevaluated my entire lifestyle. He had encouraged me to invest my savings in his father's business. I later discovered that was to secure his own position there." Aurora paused to tilt her head slightly and smile. "Now I have a few weeks to get to Colorado and find a new place to live and start my life over. Nothing to it, huh?"

Will nodded his head reassuringly but her smile had his pulse racing again. Alternate plans for her raced through his mind, and none of those plans included her living in Durango, Colorado.

He wished he knew what was going on with him. He seemed to be under some sort of spell, all due to this crazy redhead. This girl might very well be crazy to quit a good job and start her own business, but who could judge? He knew only that he liked her. He definitely liked the way she made him feel.

"The owner of the bookstore is selling because she is retiring in July. She's had a couple of other offers, but she agreed to give me first refusal, because of her long friendship with my parents. I have until July first to sign a formal contract with her and put the money on the line or the store goes to the highest bidder. Although I have a solid portfolio and look quite secure on paper, I can't access the funds until June thirtieth or I lose quite a bit of capital. That's the reason for the deadline."

"You've put a lot of thought into this." As he spoke, Will mentally reviewed the businesses in Post for possibilities.

Will's voice held no censure. Why that should matter eluded her, but it was reassuring. So many of her acquaintances had told her she was just plain nuts to leave her high-salaried job in Houston for a total—and very risky—life style change. At least Will seemed to take her plans seriously—once she'd explained them to him.

Aurora pushed a strand of hair from her face and tried to rein in the rush of feelings his proximity stirred within her. Maybe she was nuts. After all, she'd met this man only yesterday.

"I'd planned to stop in Lubbock or Amarillo next. But I guess I'll have to stay around here somewhere until I get the car situation squared away." Aurora rubbed her temples and sighed.

Will stood and grabbed his crutches. "I'll let you call your insurance agent while I get the dishes cleaned up. When that's done, I'll call the sheriff while you get some more rest."

He clomped off, and she watched him go. Disabled as he was, he still looked strong and capable—and sexy. Aurora chided herself for her wayward thoughts, retrieved her auto insurance information from the briefcase and called her agent. The insurance company office was closed for the weekend, but she left a message on the answering machine and promised to call again on Monday. That task completed, she sighed and settled back against the pillows. All the activity of breakfast, followed by talking, made her head ache. She closed her eyes and soon fell asleep.

Will awakened Aurora when he retrieved the phone from where it lay on the bed beside her. She smiled up at him from her pillow, and Will's heart pounded erratically. She moved her legs aside under the covers so he could once again sit beside her.

Her auburn hair lay spread across the pillow as she looked up at him with sleepy eyes. The neck of the over-sized pajama top revealed ivory skin to the cleft of her ample breasts. Will very much wanted to forget about calling the sheriff and just crawl into bed with Aurora. The overpowering feeling came so quickly that, for a moment, it took his breath away. Aurora, however, seemed to have no idea of the effect she had on him.

In spite of his carnal longings, Will sat on the edge of the bed in the place she had made for him. It was then that a vision of Nancy in that same spot in their bed flashed before him. Guilt poured over him. How could he have forgotten Nancy?

How could he have forgotten the pain Nancy endured lying here in this same bed? The powerless feeling he experienced as he watched his wife slip away returned. For a brief moment he thought he might have to leave the room to recover control of his emotions. He took a deep breath and fought for some semblance of restraint.

"Sorry, I tried not to wake you. This damn cast and the crutches make it hard to sneak in and out of the room quietly. I thought I'd better let the sheriff know you're safe in case a pilot spots your car."

He saw her puzzled look and explained, "It looks as if the rain may begin again any moment, but for the present it's stopped. Small planes and helicopters are already flying over the area to assess the extent of the flood damage."

Will called the Garza County Sheriff, reported Aurora safe, and gave the last known location of her car. The deputy with whom he spoke promised to alert air patrols about the car.

"Now, I need to call my daughter Kelly. She's at my mother's home in Lubbock," Will said.

"How old is your daughter?" She saw his eyes light up and a smile spread across his face at her question.

"She's ten—going on thirty. She thinks she has to take care of me since Nancy died."

"It must have been very hard on both of you, your wife dying so young."

Will clenched his jaw. "Yes. Words can't describe how hard it was . . . and is."

When Aurora saw the pain in his eyes, it made her heart ache to see how much he still cared. She didn't know whether she should probe further, but her curiosity about his life forced her to ask, "Was she in an accident?"

"No." Will took a deep breath. After three years he still found talking about Nancy's death almost too painful to bear. "She had leukemia—a kind that's almost always fatal. We didn't even realize she was ill. She'd been feeling tired for several weeks, but hadn't mentioned it to me."

He ran his hand across his face, as if to wipe away the memory. "One day when we woke up, she found herself covered in bruises. I rushed her to the doctor in Lubbock, and he did the usual tests right away." He shook his head and looked away to hide the agony the memory brought with it.

In his mind he could see once again the look on Nancy's face when the doctor told them the reason for her bruises, feel again the shock of knowing he would lose her. After a few moments, he continued.

"I didn't know leukemia could progress so quickly. Nancy only lasted two months after the diagnosis." He gazed into space as if lost in the heartwrenching memories.

Aurora had no idea how to respond, so she changed the subject as gently as she could.

"Do you and Kelly live out here by yourselves?"

Will remained lost in memories for a few seconds before he returned his gaze to Aurora. He smiled, as if in apology for momentarily shutting her out of his thoughts.

"Yeah. I have a housekeeper and the foreman's house isn't too far away, but basically it's just us."

Aurora looked around the room. "This house looks fairly new. How long have you lived here?"

"Nancy and I lived in Post until we built this house six years ago."

Aurora could visualize the newlyweds planning their dream house and the thought brought an unwelcome feeling of envy for the perfect life the two had shared. She squelched it immediately. "What about your folks? Do they still help with the ranch?"

"My father developed serious heart problems while I was in college, so he and Mother moved into Lubbock to be close to any medical care he might need. When Dad died five years ago, Mother wanted to remain in Lubbock. She hardly ever comes to the ranch or to Post. I don't think she ever really liked the isolation of ranch life."

Aurora picked up his left hand from where he rested it on the bed beside her. His strong hands fit around hers so well. This was a real cowboy, and the scars and calluses on his suntanned hands proved it.

A thin white line circled the finger where yesterday she'd

seen a ring. Before she had a chance to stop them, words came tumbling out. "You wore your wedding ring yesterday when we ate. You're not wearing it now."

He laced the fingers of his hand with hers. "That's right." Will looked at her, searching each part of her face. "I took it off when I got home yesterday."

"Why yesterday?" Aurora lay back against the pillows, her heart aflutter with a rush of feelings, her being mesmerized by those steel gray eyes which now looked right into her soul. Could he sense the chaos he caused in her thoughts, the awakening of unknown desires he caused in her body?

As if unsure how to answer her question, he looked away and took a deep breath before he answered. "Kelly has been trying to get me back into circulation, she's been pestering me to quit wearing my wedding ring."

With a shrug, he turned his gaze back to hers. "I promised Kelly that if I ever met a woman who aroused my interest, I'd quit wearing it."

Aurora's eyes widened, but she remained silent as she continued to look into Will's eyes. She didn't want to leap to conclusions, yet she found herself hoping that she understood his meaning correctly.

He kept his left hand entwined with her fingers as he leaned over her to rest his weight on his elbow, partially pinning her under him. With his right hand he pushed a lock of hair from her face. She held her breath when he let his hand travel down her cheek, then trail slowly over her throat until it came to rest on the bed near her shoulder. Her mind could hardly process the myriad of new sensations which washed over her body.

How could she feel so intensely about a man she had just met?

This is ridiculous, she told herself. *Am I not on my way to Colorado to become an independent and successful business-woman? Do I not have a nice, neat plan outlined for myself?*

Why did she have this inexcusable desire to beg him to slip into bed beside her and make passionate love to her? *Because what he's doing feels so good,* said a wicked little voice in her head. Will smiled down at her.

"When I met you yesterday, I was, well, I guess you could say fascinated." He kissed the tip of her nose and smiled down at her. "I saw you get out of your car and look around at me, and I felt like I'd been bewitched." He smiled again. "Maybe that's why I let you steal my parking spot."

His finger lightly traced her lip. "When you blew me that kiss . . . well, I can't explain the way I felt, but I knew I had to find a way to meet you."

Aurora was secretly pleased. He made her sound like some sort of siren or temptress, which certainly wasn't how she perceived herself.

In her mind, she saw herself as a cool, efficient, no-nonsense type bent on achieving her goals. Definitely impervious to the casual advances of any man. Apparently she had overestimated herself. And Will could never be classified as just *any* man. As if it had a will of its own, her hand slid up his arm while she explained her reaction to him.

"You surprised me when you sat down in that booth beside me. I was terribly embarrassed and defensive when I realized I'd stolen a parking spot from someone with a broken leg. You looked so mad, I thought you wanted to choke me."

Will ran his finger lightly across her lips again, and this time let it trace along her neck and almost to her breasts before he dropped his hand to the bed beside her. "No, that wasn't what I wanted at all."

Aurora felt herself sink further under his spell, and tried to resist. Remember your resolve, her conscience reminded her. She almost told her conscience to take a hike, but gave in to reason. In an attempt to break his spell on her, Aurora said only, "You said you were going to call your daughter."

Will took a deep breath before he picked up the phone again, and dialed his mother's phone number. Aurora loved the tone of his voice. Devotion for his daughter and mother showed with every word he spoke. She heard him laugh, heard the caring tone of voice he used, but tried not to pay too much attention to the details of his conversation.

While he spoke, she toyed with the items on the night stand beside her. Only when she caught his amused glance did she realize she had placed everything there in perfect order. Why did she have to be such a perfectionist?

To cover her annoyance with herself, she asked, "What did your daughter ask that was so funny?"

"She wanted to know if I still wore my wedding ring— that's been such an unbelievably big deal to her lately. Most kids don't want a stepmother, but she's determined to get one. I think it's because her friend Marcie's father remarried last year, and Marcie's been telling her how great it is to have a stepmother."

Will ran his fingers through his hair as he continued, "When I told her I'd taken it off, she wanted to know if it was because of you. I try never to lie to her, so I had to tell her yes. Then, she wanted to know if I plan to keep you here. That's when I said I certainly intend to try."

Aurora folded her hands primly together in her lap. "Oh, but I told you I'm on my way to Colorado."

"I know what you told me," Will said as he took her

hand. "Aurora, I let you walk out of the restaurant yesterday in Snyder without even knowing how to contact you. I went to the college to try to find you, but I didn't see your car. I felt like a fool for letting you get away."

He traced his finger across her palm. "Now that I have a second chance, I won't waste it." He revealed far more of himself than he intended at this point. His statement surprised even himself.

Before she could comment, he withdrew his hand and changed the subject. "While you were asleep I washed the clothes you took off in the laundry room." Aurora remembered that he had done most of the taking off—which was probably why he was looking at her with such interest right now.

He flashed her a wicked grin. "Although I like the way you look in that pajama top of mine, I suppose you'll be more comfortable in your own clothes—and definitely a lot safer."

Aurora looked down at her hands. "Thank you." Suddenly she felt shy and embarrassed, unsure of herself.

Will saw an unwelcome reserve slip over her expression. Damn, damn, damn! Had he revealed too many of his feelings too soon, pushed too hard? Better back off, he told himself. And keep things casual. This woman is definitely worth waiting for.

He tried to continue as though he felt more certain of himself than he actually felt. "Nick insisted that you rest, especially since your medical care has to be delayed. It's best not to take any chances, Aurora. If the roads open later, we'll go to Snyder so Nick can check your injuries. He asked me to call just before we leave so he can meet us."

"Oh. You mentioned some clothes?"

"I'll get them. Do you think you can manage a shower?"

"Yes, I'm sure I can manage a shower by myself this time." Aurora colored at the memory of Will's help the previous evening. Her body tingled as she remembered his gentle touch, the caring way he helped her.

He really was a very attractive and gentle man, but his heart still seemed to belong to his wife. She had better be careful—or she would get her heart broken once more. The last thing she needed was to be someone's second chance at love, no matter how captivating that someone might be.

She slid her feet to the floor. A brisk shower would definitely help clear her head. Or, on second thought, a bath would be even better. Aurora had always done her best thinking during a long, luxurious soak in the tub.

Chapter Five

Will's knock on the bathroom door roused her from the warm bubble bath she was enjoying. "I'm fine," she called back to him. "I'll get out now."

Will waited for her in one of the bedroom chairs until she sank thankfully to the bed. "Are you okay?" he asked as he struggled to stand on his crutches.

"Yes, I feel much better." Her heart did flip-flops again when he smiled at her. So much for thinking.

When Will picked up the bottle of hydrogen peroxide and some cotton balls, Aurora dropped the robe to her hips so he could treat her back. Though his touch might be gentle now, she knew behind the gentleness lay immense strength he had called on to rescue her from the flood. She found herself aware of each movement, each shift of his body.

Why did she find herself gazing at him, thinking of him constantly, as if she were some love-struck schoolgirl? With a sigh, she relaxed and gave in to her feelings. She might as well enjoy the moment.

He leaned closer and she closed her eyes and inhaled deeply. The scents of his soap and aftershave mingled to form a clean, masculine aroma. When she opened her eyes, she saw sandy gold chest hairs curling above the neck of his shirt. The urge to reach out and touch him almost overpowered her.

The air on her damp body coupled with his gentle touch on her back and shoulder made the nipples of her breasts harden and point. As if all at once, Will became aware of his effect on her. He paused to gently brush the corner of her mouth with his lips.

"Hmm. Nice to know you're not totally unaffected by me."

Aurora grabbed a pillow to clutch to her breast as her jaw jutted defensively. "It's—it's the cool air on my damp skin." She felt a fiery blush flash across her face.

Will finished his first aid treatment and cleared away all the paraphernalia involved to the table beside the bed. Gently, he took her face in his hand and kissed her mouth, then slid the pillow away. Aurora tried to force herself to stop him. Instead, she found herself meeting his kiss, her right hand sliding to his shoulder to pull him closer.

She moaned as she felt his tongue slip between her lips. He tasted so good. She fought again for self-control, but found herself leaning into his kisses once more. His hand slid to the small of her back, pulling her toward him.

Will fanned kisses along her neck and shoulder as his hand slid to cup her breast. Aurora clutched his hair with her hand and pulled him to her as his lips reclaimed hers. She clung to him as he lowered her to the bed.

His mouth feathered gentle kisses over her cheeks, her earlobe, and down her neck. As his mouth claimed the hard rosy nipple of her breast, she gasped. She heard her gasp become a moan at the pure pleasure his mouth induced.

His touch on her body brought joy she never knew existed. With his hands and mouth he caressed, suckled, nipped, teased until she thought she would melt. What ecstasy! Could anything else ever be as sweet as this moment? Just as she lost all sense of reason, he pulled back.

Eyes dark with passion, he gazed hungrily at her body, and leaned to kiss her lips briefly once more before pulling away. It was difficult, ending that kiss when he wanted her so very much. The problem was, he wanted much more, more than her injuries would allow.

"I think you'd better get this nightshirt on and cover up before I forget how badly you're injured." His voice rasped with the heat of the compelling desire he felt for her.

Aurora pulled the sheet over her legs and struggled into the nightshirt he offered. She knew she had been unable to put a halt to any lovemaking he might have begun. Forgotten were her injuries and pain, forgotten too was the pain of past betrayals, of her broken engagement in Houston. Forgotten were the carefully plotted plans for her future. Her only thoughts were of her need for this one man.

She had been lost in Will's spell, felt lost still as she struggled to control her breathing to meet his mesmerizing gaze. *Does he know the effect he has on me? How could I have given myself so completely to a man I hardly know? And I would have, oh, yes, I would have. Injured or not, I would have been completely his if he had not pulled away.*

Aurora put her hand on his arm. "Will, I . . . I can't imagine what's come over me. I've always been so calm and reserved. Really, I'm never like this, but I just seem to lose all sense of reason or caution with you."

Aurora put her hands to her flushed cheeks and repeated, "I still can't believe the way I acted the first time you saw me—and then I let you help bathe me last night, and . . . and just now. I don't know what's come over me."

"Mm, I think I do. I like it a lot." Will kissed the top of her head. "Now, I'll give you some privacy and check back with you in a little while."

Will worried about his ranch. He had worked hard all of his life, damn hard. Sure he could have let his foreman handle the work while he played gentleman rancher, but that wasn't his style. In the past ten years since he'd graduated from college, he had intensified his efforts to be the best rancher in the area.

It was under his guidance that the ranch had prospered, adding cutting horses, refining the beef production, expanding the hay cultivation. Putting in twelve and fourteen-hour days was normal for him, especially the past three years. And he'd accomplished all he had despite the unpredictable Texas weather.

Drought, searing heat, freezing winters, floods, sandstorms, violent winds, hail—he had survived it all and managed to turn a profit even in the lean years. He intended to continue doing just that.

Without a doubt, he would face some heavy losses from this flood. To make matters worse, the rain was falling again, though not so violently this time. He hoped the forecast for clearing weather proved correct.

His ranch complex, situated at the top of a hill, was cut off in three directions by the water. With more rain, he and Aurora would be isolated for a while longer. The other farm buildings, though safe on a nearby hill, were also surrounded by water.

Will sat on a kitchen chair. Thoughts of himself alone on this accidental island with a beautiful woman ran through his mind. Somehow, he had to make Aurora stay, and he knew he must work fast.

In the doorway across the room, Will stood with a strange expression on his face. His body clenched with tension and a longing he felt unable to explain. Aurora's presence seemed so right in this room, so natural.

When his sister Lori Beth had redecorated for him, she'd

promised to make this room his private domain. He would never have believed a woman could look so much at home in these masculine surroundings. What he had thought of as his personal retreat suddenly looked like the perfect setting for this beautiful woman.

"You're supposed to be resting, remember?"

Aurora turned with a start, then smiled. That smile lightened his heart. She still stood near the window, and the dark green background of the paisley-printed draperies brought out the green of her eyes.

"I've only been up a few minutes." She looked down at her legs, then walked over to Will. "My legs seem to work better now."

"And very nice legs they are," Will said. "I think the bruises and scrapes on the knees are an unnecessary decoration, though. But you seem to be healing well."

Aurora nodded. "Thanks to you."

Will only shrugged, but he longed to hold her, to run his hands over those long legs and up her body. He gripped the crutches tightly to prevent himself from reaching for her. If he had her in his arms at this moment, there would be no stopping his rampant desire.

She reached for the robe, but found it still damp. At least she was more covered up by the nightshirt than she had been by the pajama top she'd worn at breakfast. "Is there no end to your household talents? You cook, you clean, you do laundry."

"I'm an all-around kind of guy. And the best is yet to come. Lunch is served," Will said with a devilish grin as she brushed by him.

He'd prepared roast beef sandwiches and fruit, and set two places at the breakfast bar. Will had Kelly's portable radio turned low and he sang absentmindedly along with a country song as he poured her some orange juice. His voice had a rough, earthy quality which Aurora found both pleasing and arousing.

She hummed along for a few bars just to tease him.

He looked up in surprise. "Sorry, I do that without thinking. Didn't mean to hurt your ears. But if you don't like country music out here, you're in big trouble. That's about all the local radio stations play."

Will felt more at ease than he had at breakfast, but he was having difficulty ignoring the pert tips of her breasts which pressed against the nightshirt she wore. He ran his hand through his hair. Oh, man, this deserted island stuff was tough.

Rain was still falling, but more slowly. According to the radio announcer, the rain would move out of the area and sunshine would follow. Will speculated that electrical power would be restored by tomorrow, and perhaps the phone service also.

"I talked with the county sheriff's dispatcher. The roads aren't open yet, but might be by this evening. I called Kelly, and told my sister to wait until tomorrow to drive her home from my mom's. Everyone's pretty much stuck where they are."

Aurora looked around the room. "I think I have cabin fever. Is there an area outside where I could look around and get an idea of where we are and still stay out of the rain?"

"Sure. If you wonder why the house faces the railroad, you'll understand when you see the view from the back." Will turned to lead the way.

Following him, Aurora watched his powerful arms and shoulders as he used his crutches to help him walk. Who could have imagined she would find such a handicap so intriguing? She remembered the muscles of his upper body as they had looked last night when he'd taken off his shirt. No wonder he had been able to pull her through the torrential flood water and up the treacherous slope of the railbed.

Will reached the family room and paused to let Aurora go first. Then he hobbled over to open draperies that covered a massive wall of glass with sliding doors in the center.

Aurora gasped at the panorama before her. "Oh, Will, how wonderful. I had no idea the country around here looked like this. What a glorious view."

Will smiled proudly as he led the way to a covered patio that ran the length of the back of the house. From its covered portion, the patio extended to reach the raised sun deck surrounding a rectangular swimming pool now overflowing with rain water. Beyond that, the rolling hills and prairie stretched to the horizon, offering magnificent vistas of red bluffs streaked with buff and brown, of canyons, ravines, and grassland bounded by a creek on the right.

"I know that this landscape seems empty to a lot of people, but it's beautiful to me. I'll never tire of looking at it." Will's eyes drank in the view as if he truly would never get his fill.

Aurora instinctively understood Will's love for this land. It was a part of him greater than this house or this ranch. Once again, she felt herself sinking deeper under his spell.

"It is beautiful. That must be the river I see off in the distance." Aurora pointed to a distant ribbon of shining brown water.

"No, the river's not visible from here. What you see is another creek which flows into the river several miles beyond this one. There's usually not much water in it, sometimes none you can see from here. The river actually has several forks near here, though. This ranch is between two of the forks."

"Is that why there's so much flooding?"

"Well, partly. One of the big reasons is the raised railroad bed on which you found refuge. The water has to slowly work its way under the bridges like the one you crossed. The railroad beds stop the natural runoff of water to the streams and eventually the rivers."

"That's the Brazos River, isn't it?" Aurora tried to remember the details of the map she had of the area—the map still in her missing car.

Will nodded assent and shifted his weight to ease his left leg. "Yes, specifically the Double Mountain Fork of the Brazos. You must have crossed one of the forks yesterday before it rolled up."

"Before it what?" Not certain she heard correctly, Aurora stepped closer to him.

Will looked down at her and smiled. God, she was so beautiful with her face turned to his, her attention given to his every word. "Rolled up. When there's a heavy rain, rapid runoff creates a huge wall of water that moves down the river bed with a loud roar. The wall can be over ten feet tall and pushes aside anything that gets in its way. We call it rolling up and it's an unforgettable sight."

"It sounds frightening." Aurora remembered her near-drowning in the swollen creek and shivered.

"It is frightening, no matter how many times you see it. That much power can be very destructive." Will had seen cattle carcasses which had been swept miles from their home range.

Aurora hated to remember the flood with such a beautiful view to claim her attention, so she sat on the nearby porch swing.

Will sat beside her, then picked up her hand. It fit so well in his hand. He wanted to hold her again, to make love to her. He reminded himself of his resolution to keep things cool for awhile and struggled to sound far more casual than he felt.

"The house on your left belongs to the Hankins. Then just out of sight is Raul and Lily Chapas's house. The horse barns are right over there." He pointed. "You could take a riding tour of the ranch with me after you're feeling better and I'm rid of this cast."

"I'd like that," Aurora said warmly. "Hey, you can see both sunrise and sunset from this spot."

Will nodded, pleased by her enthusiasm.

"If the sun comes out and the clouds remain, the sunset this evening should be spectacular," Will said. This was his favorite spot to be at sunset, here or on horseback.

"I love the house, Will. The view is even nicer."

Aurora and Will rocked slowly in the porch swing, sitting a safe distance apart. They talked companionably of trivial things as the rain drizzled down beyond the sheltered area of the patio.

The air smelled wonderfully clean and fresh as it caressed Aurora's skin. The rain diminished to a fine mist, and her legs were cold. She curled them up under her, making a tent of the nightshirt. Will's ranch was truly a little part of heaven. No wonder he loved it so.

"Okay. If you want to see the sunset, you should nap first," he said, with mock sternness.

"But—" Aurora protested.

"No buts. Off you go. See you at suppertime."

She got up reluctantly, and went off without another word.

Chapter Six

Will woke with a start. He had dozed off himself. He sat up in the porch swing and frowned. Something seemed wrong, and it took him a few seconds to realize that it was the total quiet. No rain fell. The generator must have run out of fuel and stopped also. Cursing to himself, Will rose to check the machine.

In a matter of minutes he refueled and restarted the gasoline-powered generator. With only enough fuel for about ten to twelve more hours, he hoped the electrical power would be restored soon. Otherwise he'd have to siphon gasoline from one of the vehicles.

With that chore done, he started food preparation. He chuckled to himself and wondered what Aurora would make of the impromptu meal with her finicky eating habits. He had dinner almost ready when Aurora came out onto the patio.

"Sorry. I slept for a long time. Am I too late to help?" She wore the slacks and shirt Will left lying for her at the foot of the bed.

"Your timing is perfect, especially if you're hungry. I just put the steaks on the grill. The potatoes and corn on the cob are already baking. Everything else is ready."

A lantern like the one in the bedroom illuminated the table, and there was a box of matches set nearby. The same bucket he'd used last night sat on a chair. Stacked haphazardly inside the bucket were plates, cutlery and glasses. Aurora set the table while Will attended to the food on the grill.

As they sat down to eat, the sky blazed with brilliant pinks, oranges, and reds. The sun dropped through the purple clouds that streaked across the horizon and long blue shadows stretched across the earth. The sky's colors reflected on the western-facing bluffs before them, as if the sunset was dissolving into the land below it. Other bluffs wore shades of dark blue and purple as they lost the sun.

Will thought Aurora fit perfectly into the scene around them. The fading light still touched her hair. That auburn hair with lighter highlights, her purple shirt, and tan slacks matched the bluffs and the sky. She looked as one with this land he loved so much, and he vowed once more to try to keep her here—and make her a part of his life.

When she finished her meal, she leaned back in her chair to savor the beauty of the evening. "That has to be the most beautiful sunset I've ever seen."

"You can't get a sunset like this in the city. I planned it just for you, fair maiden." He took great pleasure in Aurora's company on such a beautiful evening, gratified that she appreciated the uncommon beauty of his domain.

"Well, thank you, kind sir. How very thoughtful of you. You're right. The sunsets here are spectacular. Much nicer than the ones in the city. I'll bet the stars are something to see, too." Aurora sat up and looked at Will. "Now, for the serious stuff, like what's for dessert?"

"There's ice cream surprise," Will said innocently.

Aurora looked at Will with suspicion. "What's ice cream surprise?"

"Ahh, I knew you'd fall for that old line. The surprise is that there's only ice cream. My culinary talents don't run to desserts."

"I should have seen that coming. Since you fixed dinner, let me bring out the ice cream." Aurora hoped to save Will an unnecessary trip on crutches, even just to the adjacent kitchen.

She gathered up a small load of dishes and cutlery to take with her as she went into the kitchen. There, she found the freezer packed with food.

No wonder he keeps an emergency generator, she thought. Otherwise, all this food would have spoiled. She wondered how often power failures occurred out here.

Enough twilight remained to scoop the ice cream into pretty dishes and return to the patio. Will lit the lantern as she reappeared. Some traces of the sunset were still visible as the night gently descended.

They ate their ice cream in comfortable silence until Aurora issued a great sigh. "Now I'm full. That was a wonderful meal."

"How do you stay so thin? You eat like a field hand." He decided not to point out how precisely she cut her steak. He had never seen anyone eat corn on the cob so neatly.

"That's something I get from my grandmother Aurora. I have this high metabolism, you see, and I never gain any weight. I hope my luck continues, because I'm almost always hungry!"

Will stood up. He hated for this perfect evening to end. "Let's sit on the swing again until you get ready to go inside."

Aurora stacked dishes until Will placed his hand on her arm. "Come on, that can wait. There aren't many nights like this to enjoy."

"You're right. It's a beautiful night, one of the most beautiful I can remember." The romantic part of her nature wanted to savor this time with Will. Who knew what her future held? She wanted to gather each detail of this perfect evening to store away in her heart of hearts.

She stopped in mid-step and placed her hand on his arm. "Oh, look, Will. Is that a firefly?"

He followed her gaze, then walked with her to the porch swing. "Yes. The storm must really be over. There are fireflies all around the trees by the creek and some in the yard."

He sat beside Aurora and put his arm along the back of the swing behind her, not really around her, but close enough for her to be aware of it. She felt almost shy, like a teenager on a date with a new beau.

"It's been years since I've seen a firefly. I thought they'd disappeared because of all the pesticides and pollution."

"They have in some areas, but we have them here by spring. And some nights in early summer the trees are so full of fireflies it looks as if there are twinkling lights in the trees. Kelly calls them fairy lights."

"This is a wonderful place for your daughter to grow up, isn't it?" Aurora fought the impulse to snuggle up to the man beside her, but found herself resting her head on his shoulder.

Just remember he's still in love with his wife, an inner voice told her. Well, her heart answered, how could it hurt to have this one perfect night to keep as a wonderful memory?

Will took her hand in his as he answered, "Yes. Of course, we do have some crime, even out here. But all in all, it's a good life. Even with inconveniences like losing electricity and telephones during storms, I think we're way ahead compared to any city. We still have access to cultural events and shopping in nearby urban areas without having to live with the congestion every day."

"Mm. This is so peaceful. Houston seems very far away."

There was caution in his voice as he warned, "Well, it is, Aurora. Living on a ranch is very different. Not everyone can adjust to it." He looked down at her with a mischievous gleam and added, "I think it's much nicer than Durango. I don't remember any fireflies in Durango."

Startled, she looked up at him and asked, "When were you there last?"

He chuckled. "I went skiing near there over Thanksgiving a year ago with some friends from church. We didn't see even one firefly."

Aurora glared at him. "Will Harrison, you should be ashamed. That's hardly a fair comparison."

A particularly adventurous firefly came near the patio and Aurora held her breath as she watched it dart about until it flew out of sight. She sighed, "I think I could stay here and look at the fireflies and listen to the night sounds forever, but believe it or not, I'm sleepy again."

Will looked at the luminous dial of his watch. "Right, I'll put the supper leftovers in the kitchen. The dirty dishes can wait until morning."

"Okay, I'll just carry them in and put them in water to soak."

"You carry the lantern, Aurora." He said her name so tenderly that she blushed a little. "Beautiful name," he continued. "Didn't you say you were named after a grandmother? Is she still alive?"

Aurora nodded, grateful to have something safe to talk about. "Oh, yes, and very active. She's eighty-five and still drives her car to church and her bridge games and garden club."

"And she's in Port Arthur near your parents?"

"Yes, she's a real sweetheart. I think I'm her favorite. She tries to be impartial, but I'm the only one of her descendants named for her, you see. But then, you said one Aurora was enough."

"One is perfect for me," Will said so quietly Aurora could not be certain she heard him correctly.

When the dinner dishes were cleared from the patio and the leftover food securely put away, Aurora dried her hands on the kitchen towel. "I think I'll get ready for bed now."

"Good idea. I'll check the generator one more time. It'll run out of gas before morning if I leave it running and we won't have water for breakfast. I'll stop it for now and re-start it if I wake during the night."

Aurora hurried to get out of her slacks and back into her nightshirt. She knew she should insist on moving to one of the guest bedrooms, but had neither the inclination nor the will to broach the subject to Will. He seemed so nice, if only she could trust her feelings toward him. If only she could trust his feelings toward her. If only he fit into her plans.

Quickly, she finished her bedtime preparations and slid into bed, her mind filled with misgivings. Thoughts of sharing a bed with Will increased these sensations. After all, she told herself, this is a king-sized bed, and we're rational adults. Well, at least she tried to be rational. How successful her efforts would be remained to be seen.

Will came in and undressed. This time, she looked the other way until she sensed the weight of his body on the bed. Then she turned her face to Will. The light of the lantern fell softly across her face as she looked at him, propped on his elbow and gazing at her from those beautiful stone gray eyes.

He held out his hand to her, and she twined her hand in his. He continued to gaze at her. "I'm trying to remember you're injured and a guest in my home, but you're so beautiful." He lowered his head and kissed her softly. "How have I survived without you?"

72

Aurora shook her head.

"I must be crazy. You aren't in my plans at all. I've tried to remember my rule of no personal involvement until I have my own business, to focus on my plans. But I keep forgetting when you're near."

"What if I hadn't found you again? I don't want to lose you now. I don't think I could bear it." His mouth claimed hers and Will kissed her softly. When he raised his head to end the kiss, his eyes were dark with a passion belied by his gentle touch.

Aurora touched his cheek. "You do know I can't stay here with you," she said.

"I know, although it's not what I want to hear." Suddenly, his resolve crumbled and passion won as he lowered his head to nuzzle her neck. His hand crept to cup her breast as he kissed her. He felt as if fire coursed through his veins, fire that could only be quenched by making love to this woman.

His mouth sought hers and found response. He slipped his tongue between her teeth and felt her press toward him. Only the knowledge of her injuries prevented him from crushing her back against the bed with the full strength of the desire only she could evoke.

"I need you right here, right now. It's hard to remember I can't have you, that I might hurt you."

When he would have pulled away, she clung to him. "No, don't pull away again. Hold me. Keep me near you tonight."

"Oh, Aurora, I don't ever want to let you out of my sight. Won't you stay here with me? There's plenty of room, and you could use the car whenever you wish."

"That's not possible. Think of the example you'd be setting for your daughter, of the gossip she'd hear."

Will sighed, but continued to hold her close. "You're right. Of course, you're right. When you're not so close, I realize that." He nuzzled his face against her hair, reluctant to end this intimacy with her.

"Well, I've already called my Aunt Rose and explained the situation. She wants you to stay with her, and I think the two of you will like each other. I intend to do the honorable thing and get you out of here before I lose control."

Aurora hid her smile against his shoulder. "Good idea." She spoke the truth—rational thought disappeared when he held her close. "Do you think I can find a job of some sort in Post? If I don't stay busy, I'll never be able to keep myself from trying to seduce you, cowboy."

"Now that's a mighty pleasing thought, ma'am. However, Aunt Rose is checking with her friends to see if there's a temporary job nearby for you. I asked my sister Lori Beth and her husband Tommy Joe to check with their friends tomorrow also. Aunt Rose will probably have more luck, though. She has an incredible good-old-gal network."

"Do you think I'll be able to go there tomorrow? I wouldn't want any talk about me being here that would embarrass you or Kelly."

Will brushed a strand of hair from her face. "I'll talk to Kelly. This is a small community and gossip travels fast. I hope it won't upset you, but you may as well prepare yourself."

"If my being here is going to create a lot of problems for you and your family, I'm sorry, Will. I never meant to complicate your life."

"I can handle this kind of complication." He lay back on the pillow and sighed. "Go to sleep now, before I totally lose control and make love to you."

Chapter Seven

When she awoke the next day, Will still slept. He lay on his side facing her, one arm folded back over his head and the other reaching out toward her. What would it be like to wake up beside him each morning, to reach out to him? She sighed wistfully. What a wonderful way that would be to start the day.

She blushed at her thoughts and slipped out of the bed as quietly as possible and into the bathroom, scolding herself for her wayward thoughts. There was water, so Will must have wakened in the night and restarted the generator. Instead of returning to the bedroom, she went through the door on the utility room side of the bathroom and into the kitchen.

By now, she decided, it was high time she shared the responsibilities of cooking. Although she couldn't remember the last time she prepared breakfast for a man. Well, she admitted to herself, never—unless she counted her father or her brothers. She wanted to impress Will, to repay him in some measure for interrupting his routine and invading his house. Not that he seemed to mind. She found a cookbook and started her search for ingredients and utensils.

When Will appeared in the door an hour later, he wore blue jeans and a gray print western shirt which matched his eyes. He stopped near Aurora and smiled directly at her— that breathtaking smile that made her tingle from head to toe.

"Good morning. Are those biscuits I smell?"

She felt as if the sun had just risen in the room, but she managed to return his smile. How could he look so good so early in the day?

"Yes, at least I hope so. I found a cookbook in the pantry. But I haven't actually cooked in a long time, and I'm afraid you're taking your chances this morning."

Will leaned his hips back against the counter as his hands loosely held his crutches, his eyes glued to Aurora as she set food on the table before she summoned him to breakfast.

By this time he was used to her meticulous way of eating and made no comments about the precise size of the bites of ham she cut. He would have bet she sliced each small biscuit in the exact middle and used the same amount of margarine and jam on each one she ate.

After breakfast, Aurora cleared away dishes. "I can't leave these for later, Will. The food will have dried like cement on them by tomorrow when your housekeeper comes."

Will washed and Aurora dried the dishes from breakfast and their dinner of the evening before. He chatted about ranch life and shared many stories about local characters. Soon he had Aurora laughing at his anecdotes of rural life in West Texas, many of which poked fun at himself.

Although he didn't mention his wife, Aurora worried that Will might be thinking of Nancy. He had undoubtedly shared domestic chores many times with Nancy, and doing dishes with another woman probably reminded him of it. After all, Nancy had most likely designed this fabulous kitchen herself and chosen all the furnishings. In spite of that, Aurora hoped Will thought only of the present with her.

Will checked again with the county sheriff, who declared Highway 84 once again open for traffic between Post and

Snyder. Next, Will phoned Nick, his doctor and friend, and arranged to meet him at the hospital.

Aurora gathered her belongings and got ready to go. Had she been here only thirty-six hours? She was strangely reluctant to leave.

So much had happened in those few hours. It was hard to take it all in. Her world had changed dramatically. When she dreamed of finding new experiences when she set out on her journey, she had no idea all this would happen. The flood, her lost car, her sudden change of heart—it was almost too much to comprehend. And now she was falling. . . .

Aurora brought herself up sharply. No, she could not fall in love with a man she had met only two days ago. Surely her strong emotional response to Will was in part gratitude. He had saved her life.

She snapped out of her reverie as her efficient nature resurfaced. With her few salvaged belongings secured in her briefcase and suitcase, she set the battered cases near the door awaiting her return from the visit to the doctor in Snyder. By then, Will's daughter Kelly would probably be home. This might be their last time alone.

Although Will's presence filled this house, the presence of his dead wife also lingered here. Still, Aurora felt reluctant to leave the house that had been her sanctuary, however briefly.

Will helped Aurora tidy his bedroom when he failed in his attempt to dissuade her from doing so. Even the simple task of preparing breakfast had tired her, and it showed. He could see the tightness in her face around her eyes from the pain she felt, and could see she favored her left shoulder and side. The urge to protect and cherish her overwhelmed him.

He took her gently in his arms. She heard his crutches

drop as he took her chin in his hand and raised her lips to meet his. Aurora met his kiss with renewed longing. Her arms tightened around him, kneading the muscles in his back as she pulled him closer, melding herself to his form. Their kisses deepened before Will gently broke away.

"Oh, Aurora." Will pulled her head to his chest and cradled her in his arms. Her arms slid to his waist. For a few seconds he held her in his arms as if he would never release her, then pulled back slowly. "I don't want you to leave—not now, not ever—but it's time to go. We shouldn't keep Nick waiting."

"I know. I think I'm ready, Will." She felt a deep sadness that she didn't quite understand—and couldn't quell.

They arrived at the hospital with about ten minutes to spare before they were due to meet Nick. Aurora looked at the emergency room waiting area with its stacks of old magazines and cushioned chairs.

"Is this where you'll be waiting when I'm through?"

"No, I'll just tag along with you in case I'm needed."

She arched an eyebrow haughtily. "Thank you, but I can manage on my own now."

A nurse called Aurora's name, and looked at her standing with Will. "It's hard to tell which of you is the patient." The nurse smiled and stood aside for them to enter a small examining room.

"I'm the patient," Aurora said aloud and then hissed to Will, "and I can manage by myself, thank you."

Will ignored her with an innocent smile and seated himself in the chair near the door. Aurora sat on the examining table and glared at him while she gave her medical history to the nurse.

"How tall are you?"

"Five feet, eight inches tall." Aurora gave Will another glare which he responded to with a sweet smile.

"Age?"

"I was twenty-eight on February 12."

Will managed to memorize that date before the nurse shoved him out of the examining area long enough for Aurora to change into an examining gown. But as soon as the nurse left the cubicle to look for the doctor, Will slipped back into the small room. The wise woman must have foreseen this, for she had left Aurora with a sheet tucked around her legs and hips to make up for the scantiness of the rustling paper gown.

He grinned. "Come on. I've seen you with a lot less on than that. Why so shy all of a sudden?"

Aurora chose not to dignify his rude question with a response.

Within a few minutes, the doctor walked in. The men exchanged greetings and Will stepped into the hallway to wait. Aurora liked Nick at once. His friendly tone changed to concern as he examined Aurora's bruised shoulder and ribs, and the lump on her head.

Nick gently probed the wound. "Wow. Another half inch to the center, and you'd probably have been killed." He ordered lab work and a set of cranial X-rays, as well as X-rays of her ribs and shoulder, but found no permanent damage or fractures. To Aurora's chagrin, however, Nick insisted she have a tetanus shot.

After what seemed a long time, but was in fact only a couple of hours, Aurora and Will left the hospital. They stopped to eat before starting the drive back to the ranch for Aurora's luggage.

She stared at the throng of people entering the restaurant, then looked at her own wrinkled slacks and knit top.

"I'm not dressed for this place. Could we please go somewhere else?"

Will looked around in surprise. "Oh, right. I forgot that it's Sunday. These folks are in their Sunday best. The food's good here, but I guess we do look pretty casual for this after-church crowd." Not that he cared. She looked wonderful to him, no matter what the state of her clothes.

She smiled at him. "Thanks. We could go somewhere else."

That statement lifted Will's spirits as he pulled into the Dairy Queen. "Here we are, ma'am. Money is no object. I'm feeling so generous that you can order the most expensive thing on the menu if your little heart so desires."

Aurora laughed at the fun he poked at the popular dine-in or take-out restaurant found in almost every Texas town. She felt so at ease with him right now. It seemed as if she had known him for years and years.

Once inside, Aurora felt ravenous. She ordered chicken-fried steak fingers and gravy, with french fries and a root beer. Will ordered the same thing but questioned the benefits to their health. "Here you go again. Your cholesterol count must be up there!"

"Actually, it's quite low. I don't usually indulge in quite so much fried food, though. My experiences of the past few days have left me feeling reckless—or maybe it's your presence. I told you I seem to lose all sense of caution with you around."

"Well, ma'am, I like to think I'm a good influence whenever possible. I seek to introduce flexibility and frivolity wherever I go. And I fight against the evil forces of rigidity and prudence."

"Wow. Thank you, caped crusader."

With her container of cream gravy placed in just the

right spot next to the basket of food, she cut a one-inch piece of steak to dip into the gravy. When she had eaten that, she cut another of precisely the same size and started the process again.

Fascinated, Will watched each motion. "Well, this is even more unbelievable than watching you reorganize your hamburger in Snyder or slice your ham at breakfast." He had never met a person so intensely in control of her actions.

Aurora looked crestfallen. "Maybe my former fiancé was right. Russell used to say I was an overly-organized perfectionist." She looked at Will decisively and picked up the container of gravy. With one plop, she dumped the gravy onto the mound of fried steak strips and leaned back triumphantly. "How's that?"

Will laughed. "That's good, Aurora. Now you're living dangerously." This unpredictable woman made his heart feel sixteen again.

Aurora cut a bite of gravy-covered steak strip and chewed it, and pretended to look surprised. "Hey, it tastes just the same as the other way."

When they returned to the ranch, it was to find Will's sister and brother-in-law waiting there with Kelly. Quickly, Aurora straightened her hair and smoothed her clothes with her hands. Her palms felt damp with apprehension.

She chided herself. After all, there was no reason to be nervous. Why was it so important that these particular people like her? She mustered her courage, took a deep breath, and walked into the kitchen with a smile on her face.

Lori Beth was a very feminine version of her older brother. She wore a slate blue linen maternity suit that matched her laughing blue eyes and complimented her sandy hair. Her husband Tom had removed his jacket and tie, and wore dark slacks with a white shirt open at the throat.

A little girl in a frilly pink dress rushed to Will. She hugged Will, then hopped from one foot to the other as she spoke to Aurora. "Wow, you're even prettier than I imagined!"

She took Aurora's hand and her eyes never left Aurora's face. Aurora smiled and Will looked embarrassed. Lori Beth and Tom seemed to enjoy Will's discomfort.

"Well, thank you, Kelly. You look very pretty yourself. Is that one of your new dresses?"

Kelly looked down at the dress she wore and smoothed the skirt with her hands. "Yes, but I like jeans much better."

Will's sister stepped forward. "I'm Lori Beth, Will's sister. This is my husband Tommy Joe. We live on the next ranch southeast of here."

"It's nice to meet you. Guess we all sort of got caught by the flood," Aurora said, feeling a bit awkward.

"Oh, the rain wasn't nearly as heavy in Lubbock as it was here. We heard on the radio that you had over ten inches. Could that be right?" Lori Beth asked her brother.

"At least that much, and mostly within two hours. Some places are still isolated by the high water."

Aurora shuddered. "Almost as bad as a hurricane."

She addressed Lori Beth and Tom. "I grew up near the coast in Port Arthur, so I've driven in heavy rains before. But I've never seen rain like that."

"You've had a terrible time. I hope it doesn't turn you against Garza County," Lori Beth said.

"Actually, I think this is a beautiful area. I'd like it a lot more with a little less water, though."

Tom laughed and Lori Beth took Aurora's hand in both of hers. "We've got to run but we'll see you again soon. You'll like Aunt Rose. She'll run your life for you if you're not careful, though. Don't be intimidated by her little ways—she really is a sweetheart."

Will shook his head and smiled. "Don't worry. I think Aunt Rose has met her match this time, Lori Beth."

When her aunt and uncle had gone, Kelly turned her full attention to Aurora. "Do you think they'll find your car? Daddy said it thought it was a boat and sailed away."

Aurora sighed and shook her head. "I don't know, Kelly. I'm afraid it'll be ruined even if it is found. I'll just have to get another one, I guess, and try to replace the things that were in it."

"Like what?" the curious little girl asked.

"Well, there were lots of clothes and shoes, my camera, maps, and a few souvenirs. There were also my favorite books, an iron, a hair dryer—you know—those things we women just can't live without."

Kelly giggled. "Now you'll have to go shopping, won't you?"

Aurora returned her smile and put her arm around Kelly's shoulders. "I guess I will, eventually."

Will looked at his watch. "We'd better get going. Aunt Rose doesn't tolerate tardiness, does she, Kelly?"

Kelly laughed at her father's remark and explained to Aurora. "She's a schoolteacher, and she's always on time. Well . . . she used to be a teacher, but now she's my school principal."

"Isn't that awkward—having your great-aunt for your principal?" Aurora asked.

Kelly looked thoughtful before answering. "No. Well, I

guess it would be if I ever had to go to the principal's office because I was bad. Aunt Rose told me that if I ever got in trouble she would punish me once as the principal and once as my aunt"—she looked at her father who in turn looked at Aurora and winked—"and then Daddy would punish me, too, when she told him."

Aurora laughed. "I guess that's enough incentive to be good at school, isn't it? Both of my parents are teachers, so I do sympathize with you, Kelly. Do you like school?"

"Oh, yeah. I'm on the honor roll, too. I think I'm ready for summer now, though. I want to have more time to ride Misty." Kelly looked at Aurora and explained, "Misty's my pony. Would you like to go see her?"

"Another time, Kelly," Will cut in. "Right now, we have to get into the car and go see your Aunt Rose or suffer the consequences later."

Chapter Eight

After hearing Will speak of his Aunt Rose, Aurora expected to meet a stereotypical sweet, plump, gray-haired, little old lady. What a surprise to be greeted by a tall, elegant woman in her late fifties. Rose's soft brown eyes gleamed with intelligence, and her rich brown hair showed only slight touches of gray at the sides.

As the principal for the middle and elementary schools, Rose Webster evidently put up with nonsense from no one. Well, almost no one. Clearly, both Will and his daughter received very special treatment in her household. Aurora found herself glad to be on this woman's good side. She imagined Rose would make a formidable opponent.

Rose's smile was gracious, and warm. "Welcome, Aurora. I hope you can climb stairs all right. The spare bedrooms are on the second floor."

"That's kind of you. I'm sure I can manage."

"Good. Kelly, please take Miss O'Shaughnessy's things up to the front bedroom." Rose patted her great-niece on the head and turned to Aurora. "Perhaps you'll help me get dinner ready and on the table. Will, you stay out of the way. Go into the living room and prop that leg up while you read the Sunday paper."

Rose indicated an old photograph of a young couple stiffly posed for the camera. "My grandparents built this house in 1923. Except for an occasional trip abroad and the time I was away at college, this is the only house in which I've ever lived."

"I really like this house, Rose. It has such a warm, welcome feeling."

Rose almost beamed. "I've traveled almost every summer of my adult life and I seem to have filled the house with souvenirs of those travels. It's cluttered but it pleases me."

Every flat surface Aurora could see displayed at least one museum-quality item. "I agree. It's a fascinating mix of objects. But doesn't it take forever to dust?"

Rose nodded goodhumoredly. "I have to confess that a cleaning woman comes every Thursday. She probably doesn't enjoy my treasures as much as I do, but she doesn't complain."

Aurora inhaled the comfortable smells of furniture polish and delicate lavender, which mingled with the tempting aroma of their dinner. She guessed they were having roast beef and potatoes and recognized the cinnamon-and-apple scent of warm apple pie. Aurora stood for a few moments taking it all in before she noticed Will's smile.

"Well, so I'm relegated to the living room while you and Aunt Rose slave away in the kitchen." Will hobbled across the living room to sit in the large blue armchair near the fireplace. He raised his cast to adjust his leg for maximum comfort on the ottoman in front of the chair before he reached for the newspaper.

Aurora stood with arms akimbo. "You don't exactly look heartbroken, Will. I think you're used to Rose spoiling you."

Will settled himself in the chair and opened the front section of the newspaper. His eyes twinkled and he flashed one of his dazzling smiles. "You're so right. I didn't intend to imply that I'm in any way complaining."

This was a new side of this complicated man. She could

easily imagine him as he had been when visiting his aunt as a child. How docile he looks, Aurora thought. She suddenly pictured herself in the large chair facing Will, crackling logs in the fireplace giving off warmth on a wintry evening, each of them reading one of the books from the bookcases that flanked the mantel.

You dolt, this is not even his house. Get hold of yourself. You know you have plans which do not include Will Harrison. Aurora gave herself a mental shake and followed Rose into the kitchen. She was beginning to get comfortable in his territory. The sooner she got on her way to Colorado, the better.

"Will tells me you had quite an ordeal this weekend"— Rose carved slices of the roast and placed each slice onto a serving platter as she carved—"and you might need a few days to recuperate before you start work. Is that right?"

Aurora nodded.

"Will's friend, Dr. Nick Linder, said to take things easy for a couple of days until the headaches subside. I should be ready to work by Wednesday or Thursday. Do you have something lined up already?" Rose's good-old-girl network must really work as fast as Will indicated, Aurora thought.

"I have something in mind. Perhaps I should see if you'd be interested before I pursue it." Rose finished carving the roast and cleaned the carving knife. She slid the knife into the proper slot of the wooden holder on the counter with a precision that made Aurora feel very much at home.

"Frankly, I'm worried about my friend Peggy's health. Your unexpected detour could be a godsend for her." Rose handed the meat platter to Aurora. "Take the meat through, please, and I'll bring the vegetables." She looked around in exasperation. "What is keeping Kelly?"

Aurora found that working with Rose was like keeping up with a whirlwind. Kelly came into the kitchen as Aurora exited to the dining room. Rose issued staccato instructions to the little girl before following Aurora. With all the food on the table and the settings arranged to her satisfaction, Rose called Will to join them for dinner.

During dinner, Rose revealed her plan to Aurora. "My friend Peggy runs the card and gift shop in town, but her business has declined the past few years. Her health is failing and she's not really up to running a small business. That's where you would come in, Aurora. She can't postpone surgery any longer."

Will looked at his aunt, a speculative light in his eyes. This might work out. A card and gift shop was similar enough to a bookstore in size and ease of operation. "Aurora needs the job. She has to buy a new car—they never found the Mustang."

Rose continued briskly. "And they never will. Now Will says you have a marketing degree and you've got a good head for business." Aurora flashed Will a look of surprise. He had no way of knowing whether she was a good businesswoman or not—or of confirming what she'd told him. He beamed at her while his aunt continued.

"Peggy's shop is on the main street of Post. Quite a nice location to my mind. Would you be willing to manage the place while she has surgery and recuperates?"

Aurora felt a momentary panic at being put on the spot by this no-nonsense woman regarding a shop she had never seen. Her professional confidence soon resurfaced. "Well, it sounds like it might be on-the-job training for the bookstore I've been thinking of buying. Will may have told you, though, that I'm on my way to Colorado. What sort of time frame do you have in mind?"

Rose looked thoughtful for a moment. "Well, if you start on Wednesday or Thursday, Peggy can spend the rest of this week showing you how she wants things done. Possibly she could have her surgery Monday or Tuesday of next week. She'll be able to return to work in four weeks."

As she leaned forward, Rose placed her hand on the table. "Aurora, if you can convince Peggy you can handle the shop, you'll be doing her a great service. It will also ease my mind and that of her other friends. She's postponed this surgery for over a year and has suffered terribly for it."

Kelly asked, "What's wrong with her, Aunt Rose?" Aurora wondered the same thing.

"It's not something to talk about at the dinner table, Kelly. She's having what we used to call 'female problems' but she wouldn't appreciate me going into details about something so personal."

Aurora thought aloud as she offered, "Hmm, Mother's Day is this Sunday and then there are June graduations and weddings coming up before Father's Day next month. Don't you think she wouldn't want to be away at this time of year?"

Rose heaved a great sigh. "Unfortunately, she thinks she's indispensable at any time. Meanwhile, she gets weaker and weaker and less able to take care of the store or herself. Leave Peggy Hopkins to me! If you agree to help, I won't let her miss the opportunity."

Aurora felt excitement rising within her. "Well, I'd love to manage a shop like that. If you can convince your friend to let me try, I'll tackle it. I don't have to be in Colorado until the end of June."

"Good. That would give you about a week to spare." Rose looked satisfied, but not as satisfied as Will. He had won a four-week reprieve in his attempt to keep Aurora in

Post. His mind set to work with other plans to get Aurora into his life permanently. He could picture her in his home—their home—preparing meals for him, a baby balanced on her hip while Kelly fed a toddler nearby. Into his mind flashed a picture of Aurora as he had seen her in his bed, hair spread on the pillow as she invited him to join her. Heat spread to his loins and he reached for his water glass. Cold water was definitely called for. Too bad he could only drink it. A shower would be more appropriate.

Unaware of his wandering thoughts, Aurora chewed on her lip a moment as she considered Rose's offer. "Doesn't your friend have someone working at the shop who could take over for her? Won't someone be offended that she's brought in an outsider?"

Rose looked shocked at the thought. "No. Oh, my goodness, no. Mattie Evans works for Peggy full time but, frankly, Mattie can just barely stock and ring up sales. At that, I suspect she makes a lot of mistakes."

Control of his mind regained, Will interjected, "I'm surprised she even finds her way to work each day."

Rose shot him a glare and continued. "Then there's Susan Stevens, who's a nice young woman, but she only works part-time. Susan is a widow with small children and needs just a little extra money to supplement the income from her husband's estate. Her mother is not all that well but keeps the children on the days Susan works. No, I'm afraid neither Mattie nor Susan is qualified to keep things going without supervision."

Rose smiled and picked up her fork. "I think this will be the perfect solution. I'll talk to Peggy after school tomorrow." Dismissing the matter as settled, she turned to Kelly. "Now, tell me what you've been up to."

Be My Guest

★ ★ ★ ★ ★

Working with Peggy Hopkins proved the most frustrating job experience of Aurora's life. Aurora's few tentative suggestions were met with instant disapproval by both Peggy and her devoted assistant Mattie.

It soon became obvious that Peggy Hopkins wanted *no* changes of any kind—especially from a young woman half her age.

"My dear, we don't expect innovations or major changes here. Just keep on with business as usual while I'm gone. Mattie will be able to show you how we arrange our displays."

Taking the rebuff in stride, Aurora said only, "This is such a perfect site for your shop. You must be so proud to have been in business with all the changes in the town." To herself, Aurora added *lucky*. The store hadn't been updated or renovated in at least a decade.

Peggy grimaced. "My friends *had* always been loyal customers, but now that the big mall in Lubbock is open some of them have forgotten this store. It seems more and more of them are deserting me." That Peggy had lasted in business this long must be due only to the loyalty of very good friends. Loyalty went only so far with the lure of better merchandise so near.

Aurora patiently learned as much as possible about the mechanics of operating the store exactly as Peggy instructed. Oh, but it went against her instincts to see a potentially wonderful store so neglected. Whether in a bustling metropolis like Houston or a dusty West Texas town like Post, Aurora liked the challenge of running a business.

As Aurora had anticipated, Peggy told her that the stock of cards, gift wrap, and other items carrying the card company name and logo had to be purchased. Those seasonal items not sold were the property of the store, and could not be returned to the card company for even partial credit. That made good marketing and careful buying even more crucial. From the shabby look of the store and the shelves full of back inventory, Aurora could see that its owner knew nothing about either.

She shook her head once more as she looked around at the cluttered shelves and unattractively arranged merchandise. Peggy was her own worst enemy. Suffering from the fatigue and discomfort of her medical problem, she could barely manage to get through the day. Perhaps Peggy no longer even noticed the dust or faded displays.

Saturday evening found Aurora mentally and physically exhausted, but with a good feeling about her ability to manage the store. She was already planning improvements and new displays, even on a short-term basis.

Over dinner Saturday evening, she relayed her feelings to Rose and Will. Aurora talked with excitement about the improvements she could make in the store with no additional expense and only a little extra effort.

"It's small but it could be such a *great* store if we got in the newer lines they sell at the mall. As it is, it can still be a good store. A good cleaning and some extra light tubes in the fixtures will help a lot."

Although happy to see the excitement that sparkled in her eyes, Will had misgivings about any changes Aurora was planning. It would be a wasted effort as far as he could see.

"Well, you survived three days with Peggy Hopkins without losing your temper. That's more than I could do." Will shook his head, then looked sheepish when he realized what he'd said about his favorite aunt's best friend.

Rose looked at her nephew with astonishment. "Why, Will, I had no idea you felt that way about Peggy!"

"I'm sorry, Aunt Rose, that sort of slipped out. But, I have always thought she was a total dingbat! I never understood how the two of you could be such lifelong friends— you're such opposites."

"Perhaps that's why we're friends. When her husband was alive, though, she wasn't quite as much of a *dingbat* as you call it. I think Harvey's death left her at a total loss." Rose tapped her fingernails on the table. "My, my. That was ten years ago. She depended on Harvey so much to help her with decisions. And now she's facing this surgery all alone."

Rose studied Aurora for a moment before continuing. "Please promise you'll stay, Aurora—for as long as she needs you."

Aurora looked at Rose and then at Will, and then she nodded. "I'll do my best."

Chapter Nine

Aurora found her first day without Peggy at Raphael's pleasant and uneventful except for the lack of cooperation from Mattie.

When Will phoned that evening, Aurora told him, "I think I'll do her bodily harm the next time she tells me how they've *always* done things before. And she makes so many mistakes that I spend half my time unraveling her errors. What an annoying woman!"

He chuckled. Personally, he thought Mattie was dumb as dirt. "Well, Peggy's surgery isn't until tomorrow. Maybe you shouldn't try to make any changes. Just stick with the status quo until Peggy comes back. It'll be a lot easier."

"But I can't stand it, Will. It could be such a great shop. With only a few changes I could make a lot of difference in her sales volume."

"Still, you don't need to revamp the place if you'll only be there such a short time. Peggy will resent it."

Aurora sounded puzzled. "I can't do less than my best. Surely you can understand that."

"Yes, but you're probably only causing hard feelings. Just coast along until Peggy comes back. If she doesn't want to make a profit, that's her business. Why kill yourself for nothing?" If he had his way, Aurora would be out of the card shop and into his home anyway. And into his bed.

"Will Harrison, I resent your lack of trust in my ability! I'm the one who's responsible for the shop's performance and

I'll do what I think best. How you can suggest I do otherwise is beyond me."

"Because it's pointless. You want to show Peggy what great ideas you have, the magic of marketing, and how to sell a heating pad in hell. But I can guarantee you that when Peggy returns she'll change everything back to exactly the way she left it."

Aurora's temper erupted. "I see. You think this is just some sort of ego trip, so I can show up the poor little country lady?"

Will's tone became placating. "Now, I didn't mean that at all." He sensed this conversation slipping completely out of his control and wondered where he had put his foot in his mouth. He only wanted to save her a lot of overwork and bruised feelings.

Her clipped words had the phone receiver almost sizzling. "It certainly sounded like that's what you meant. I gave my word to do my best. That's exactly what I intend to do."

"Don't be so stubborn. I'm only trying to save you unnecessary trouble."

"Stubborn? Me? Well, that does it. Good night, Will."

"Aurora? Aurora?" Will spoke to an empty line. He replaced the receiver on the cradle and ran his fingers through his hair. Damn, she certainly was stubborn!

Of course, it was true enough that the same had been said about him. He supposed he should let her work herself to exhaustion if that's what she wanted. He just couldn't resist wanting to take care of her.

A warning voice in his brain reminded him that he had absolutely no right to do so, and she had made that all too clear just now. If he had his way, though, he would be able to take care of her someday, to safeguard and shield her from the harshness of the world. He could be her buffer as he had been for Nancy.

All Aurora's work now would be for nothing when Peggy came back. Peggy would indeed put everything back the first morning she returned—everything but the dirt and dust, anyway. But time would take care of that soon enough.

Mattie paced and Aurora watched the clock. Three o'clock. Rose should have called them long before now. Peggy's surgery at seven should have been over long ago. Well, perhaps Rose had taken the opportunity to visit Will's mother.

The tinkle of the bell on the shop door brought both Mattie and Aurora to attention. As soon as Aurora saw the look on Rose's face, she knew Rose brought bad news. She rushed forward to greet her at the front of the store, but Rose held up her hand to quell any questions.

The older woman looked as if she had aged several years in this one day. "Could we go back to the office, dear, and sit down?"

"Of course." Aurora led Rose to the office at the back of the store and Mattie followed anxiously behind them. Aurora pulled out the chair of her desk. "Sit here and I'll start the electric kettle for tea."

Rose held up a hand. "No, no tea. I've had enough caffeinated beverages today to float a battleship."

Both Mattie and Aurora gave Rose their full attention as she settled herself in the chair and took a deep breath. "As you may have guessed, things did not go as well as expected this morning."

Mattie's face paled even more. "Is Peggy all right? She didn't . . . she's not . . . ."

Rose patted Mattie's arm. "She's going to be all right. Its just going to take a lot longer than we had imagined. The operation went very well, but Peggy's heart began fibrillating just as they were taking her to the recovery room."

It was Aurora's turn to sit down. She reached for the chair in the small eating area. "You mean she had a heart attack after the surgery?"

"Something like that, yes. I was so upset and flustered that I'm afraid some of the details may be a bit jumbled in my mind. I went into Lubbock this morning to see Peggy before the surgery. I wanted to tell her that I would be waiting and praying with her minister at the hospital."

"Is she conscious yet?" Mattie stood in the doorway, wringing her hands, as she continually glanced toward the front of the store to watch for customers.

"Peggy's in intensive care now, but she did wake up just before I left the hospital to come here."

Aurora stood up and ushered Mattie to the only other chair in the small area. "You sit here, Mattie, and I'll stand in the doorway and watch for customers." To Rose, she said, "People have been calling for several hours to ask about Peggy. What shall we tell them?"

"She'll probably go to the cardiac wing tomorrow. Then she'll have to stay in the hospital for a week or two. After that, she'll have to go to a nursing home until she's able to stay alone."

Rose rubbed her hand across her forehead in fatigue. She raised her eyes to meet Aurora's. "Oh, Aurora, I'm sorry. It's going to be a little longer before Peggy can return to the store. Even then, she'll have to take things easy."

"Oh, poor Peggy!" Aurora said instantly. Then, the realization of what this meant for her sank in. "Oh, Rose, how much longer?"

"We won't know for another week or so. I know this will really push you up against your deadline, but please don't abandon us without thinking about it. It may still work out all right."

Aurora was a woman of her word, but she was also concerned about wearing out her welcome with Rose. From the beginning, she insisted on paying Rose for her room and board. It had to be somewhat of a burden for Rose to have her there. After all, Rose valued her privacy, and had only volunteered to have Aurora with her to indulge her favorite nephew and, perhaps, to help her friend Peggy.

Aurora broached the subject to Rose one evening a couple of days after Peggy's surgery when she and Rose discussed Peggy's convalescence.

"Rose, I've been thinking you might be less inconvenienced if I found a motel or somewhere else to stay. I know you were helping Will when you offered to let me stay with you."

"Nonsense. Why, I'd be terribly offended if you moved elsewhere. I enjoy having you here"—a knowing twinkle shone in Rose's eyes—"and I must say I've never seen so much of my nephew as I have since you've been here. I always regretted that I never married and had children, so consider yourself adopted for now. Will won't mind."

"Oh." Aurora didn't know what to say.

"Most people thought I was too devoted to my career to marry—or something like that. I confess I usually do nothing to enlighten people. Oh, I don't mean to complain, mind you. Between my teaching and all of my travels, I've had a rich and varied life."

Rose looked around the room as if searching, her hand toying with a button on her blouse. "I've always wondered, though. I think I would have been a good wife and mother. You see, the truth is, the only man I ever really loved married someone else."

Rose looked into the distance wistfully a few moments before she became her old crisp self once more. "Well, that's neither here nor there. The fact is, though, that I've enjoyed having you here."

Something puzzled Aurora. "Surely Peggy would have had this surgery soon? I mean, even if I hadn't come along?"

Rose looked embarrassed. "Well, to tell you the truth, I'm indebted to you even more than Peggy. When school ended for the summer, I considered running the store myself." Rose's eyes lit up and she laughed.

"But I knew it wasn't a good idea. I don't know the first thing about running a business, but I didn't know what else to do to help out. You can see why I'm especially grateful to you. Also, who knows when Peggy's heart problem would have surfaced? If she hadn't already been in a hospital, she might have died. So, you see, you've actually saved her twice. And I hope you'll plan on sharing my home as long as you're in Post. It's the least I can do in return."

"Thank you, Rose. You don't know how much I appreciate that." Aurora's gratitude to Rose did not displace the uneasy feeling of being caught in a net which was tightening ever closer around her.

It was Will who broke the news to her a week later. She knew something serious weighed on his mind when she saw him enter the shop. He failed to notice all the changes she had made. He seemed to see nothing but her, and his face looked so severe.

Without question she followed him back to her little office for some measure of privacy and closed the door. She sat in the chair at her desk and pulled the other chair near hers.

When he agreed to accompany Rose to visit his mother in Lubbock, he realized Rose also intended to include a visit to Peggy. Loathe to navigate the halls of the hospital on crutches, he waited at his mother's home while the women visited their friend. Rose and his mother were fortunate enough to time their visit to coincide with that of the doctor.

Now he leaned his crutches against Aurora's desk and sat in the chair facing her. He had worried about this all the way from Lubbock. Would she throw her hands up and bolt or would she stay? Would she blame him for trapping her or would she welcome the additional time to be near him?

"What is it? Has someone died?"

"No, it's not quite that bad." He placed her hand in his and took a deep breath. He wished he could just hold her in his arms and protect her somehow against this blow to her plans.

"Rose and Mom talked to Peggy's cardiologist today. Peggy had a heart attack last night."

"A heart attack? After all she's been through? Will she be all right?"

Lord, give me courage and the right words. His eyes sought hers, willing her to understand. "Aurora, honey, this means she won't be able to come back to the shop in time for you to get to Colorado by July first." He saw her shock when the meaning of his words finally sank in.

She withdrew her hand and turned away. How could this happen? And she had promised Peggy she would stay. Her eyes flew to the large yearly-planning calendar over her desk.

"When will she be able to return?"

"I'm not certain. No one is right now." Personally, he doubted Peggy would ever regain the stamina needed to run her business, but he feared voicing that opinion at this point. Better to stick with exactly what the doctor said. "The doctor thought she could move to a nursing home here in a couple of weeks and then she could go home maybe four weeks after that."

"No, that can't be. It just can't." Aurora turned to face him, her eyes brimming with unshed tears. Her chance to own her own business at a price below market value might be lost forever. Yet this meant more time with this wonderful man. Even now she longed for him to take her in his arms, comfort her, caress her. She struggled to focus on the problems his news created.

"Oh, Will, that ruins all my plans. What should I do?"

"You know what I want you to do. I've already told you I want you to stay here."

He ran his hands through his hair and sighed. "I know you want to go to Durango and buy that bookstore. And I also know that, going or staying has to be your decision. But in my heart, I can't imagine life without you here."

"I don't know what to do. The Durango bookstore is a once-in-a-lifetime opportunity. But I gave Peggy my word, and that's not something I take lightly." At least Will had come to tell her in person. Thoughtful as always.

He leaned on the desk and looked at the calendar. "Is there a chance the friend in Durango would give you extra time?"

"Probably not. She has a cruise already scheduled for the middle of July to celebrate her retirement. I was supposed to spend two weeks with her to familiarize myself with the shop and clientele before she left on her cruise." She wrung her hands before he took them in his.

Her eyes once again sought his. "Unfortunately, there are two other people interested in buying the shop."

He pulled her onto his lap, balancing her gently so that most of her weight fell onto his strong right leg. "I'm so sorry. Even though I want you to stay here, I know how upsetting this must be to you."

She protested, "Will, your cast." Before she could say more, his lips were on hers. Her arms slid around his neck but she broke the kiss. He couldn't know how difficult it was not to give in to her desire for him.

"This isn't fighting fair." Yet it was what she had longed for only minutes before.

"I know. Life isn't fair." He pushed an auburn curl from her face with a caress. "Believe me, I meant it when I said the decision has to be yours. Well, at least I've tried to mean it. I fought with myself all the way here from Lubbock. Should I beg you to stay or keep my mouth shut?"

"Then which is this?"

He gave her a crooked grin. "Maybe a little of each. I'm not saying anything. I just want to balance the scales in my favor a little if I can."

He brought his lips to hers and teased her lips apart. Such sweet bliss. She gave up, at least temporarily, the fight for reason and logic. Her reasoning mind shut down and passion took charge.

She had no knowledge of her buttons coming undone until she felt his hand push away her blouse and bra. His lips captured the nipple of her breast and tugged. She heard a moan escape her lips. He stood with her in his arms.

A large hand swept aside papers on her desk and he set her down on the desk top. He kicked her chair to one side and placed himself between her legs. She arched back and his mouth captured the other breast. Somehow, her skirt seemed to be all around her waist. Will fumbled with the top of her panties and his hand found its way inside to stroke her. She grabbed his shoulders to pull him toward her, to urge him to the most intimate of caresses.

Her hands slid to his waist, then found the zipper on his jeans. Trembling fingers fumbled with the buckle of his belt. She wanted this man as she never believed possible. She wanted him now, here.

A timid knock came at the office door. "Aurora? Aurora?" It was Mattie's querulous voice.

Will's head came up and he emitted a low growl. "I swear I'll kill that woman!"

He stepped aside and leaned against the door to prevent Mattie from opening it. Gently, he zipped his jeans over his arousal, well aware that only Mattie's interruption prevented him from taking Aurora right there on her desk.

This was not at all how he had planned this. He wanted her even more than ever, but he wanted their first time together to be at his home, in his bed. He wanted to be able to take his time, to love her again and again. He wanted her to choose him over some bookstore in Durango, for God's sake. Or this card shop.

How the hell did things get this far here in her office? The door didn't have a lock—anyone could have walked in on them. He buttoned his shirt and tucked it into the waistband of his jeans. Hell, he didn't even have any protection with him.

Aurora pulled her blouse together, still gasping in great, heaving breaths. She tried to make her voice sound normal. "What is it, Mattie?"

The older woman's voice came through the closed door.

"I seem to have broken one of the little ceramic angels from the front display shelves."

"I'll be there in a little while. Make sure there are no pieces left on the floor or anywhere else. A customer might get hurt." She stood and straightened her clothing. When she stepped to the little mirror, the reflection there shocked her. Her lips were swollen, her face flushed, her hair in disarray, her clothing rumpled.

Will ran his hands over his face. "Look, I never meant things to get this far in here. I really intended just to break the news of Peggy's delayed recovery and leave you to make a rational decision on your own."

"I didn't exactly beat you off, Will. If I remember correctly, my hands were as busy as yours." She scooped up the crutches which had fallen unheeded at some time in their attempted lovemaking. "I have a tough decision to make, though. I think I need some time without you to distract me. Lord knows I can't seem to think a rational thought with you near."

When he took the crutches he grabbed her hand and pulled her to him. "I can't bear to think of you leaving. Please consider that life can't always be lived by time schedules. Give me a chance." He brushed her lips lightly and ran a finger along her cheek in a final caress before he left, closing the door gently behind him.

Aurora pushed her chair to her desk and sat down. When she saw the mess of papers on her desk she felt a flush rise to her cheeks. She placed her elbows on the desk and her face in her hands. Once again, she knew she could not have stopped their lovemaking. In Will's embrace, she forgot her plans, her goals. In truth, she forgot her own name.

How could this have happened? She had made such careful plans. Everything was set to proceed. She would get to Colorado with enough money to find a place to live, and she would have time to move the furniture from her condo in Houston. She would have time to withdraw her mutual funds on June 30 before she signed papers on July 1 to buy the bookstore. She would have two weeks to train before she was left on her own. She would become a successful store owner, find a perfect life, eventually marry the perfect man, have several perfect children, live happily ever after. A perfect plan, except that now it had just gone way off course.

She realized that she owed Will her life, and she supposed that extended to his family. Certainly, Rose had treated her as if she were a member of the family. Oh, Lord, she thought, I gave my word to Peggy, too, that I would be at the store until she could return. I promised. How can I go back on my word?

Nevertheless, she wished she could remind everyone that they had agreed on four weeks and not a day longer. *You committed to help out so that Peggy would have the surgery she desperately needed. Now you are obligated to remain until Peggy can return to work. You are trapped, my dear, neatly trapped!*

Well, one thing proved true. At least this would give her enough experience to see if this was the type of small business she wanted to establish for herself, by the time Peggy returned to work.

Aurora had to admit she wouldn't mind the extra time with Will. That thought in itself did not reassure her. She viewed her growing attraction to Will Harrison with something akin to panic. Why did she feel so happy and secure in his presence? Why did a touch from him cause her mind to shut down and let lust take over? It bothered her that any man could affect her that much.

How could she even think of leaving him now? This was

not mere lust she felt. This was something far greater. *Face it, Aurora, you are deeply in love with this cowboy,* she told herself.

Until today, when Will told her of the delay in Peggy's recovery, he had never referred to Aurora's future travels. When she had brought up the subject, he always said something noncommittal and managed to turn the conversation to another subject. She knew he did so today to try to be as fair to her as he could. How could she not love this man?

Aurora straightened the papers on her desk and opened her laptop computer. With great concentration and carefully considered wording, she composed a very difficult letter to her friend in Colorado. She would not try to hold her friend to their agreement. She had to let her know how things now stood. It seemed only fair. If things didn't work out here, there were bound to be other businesses in Colorado—or wherever she chose to live.

Chapter Ten

Aurora soon fell into a routine, and she found the days passed very quickly. She developed a good rapport with Susan. Even Mattie shocked her by grudgingly volunteering that the store seemed much improved with the changes Aurora initiated. In addition, Aurora found herself enjoying the day-to-day activities of business in a small town.

She attended Chamber of Commerce meetings, acting in Peggy's behalf, and became acquainted with many of the other business people in town. Her outgoing personality and her efficient manner made new friends for Raphael's as well as for herself. People she met about town dropped by to chat with her and usually bought at least a card while in the store.

Aurora decided to make Tuesday her day off and let Susan and Mattie manage on their own for that one day each week. On the first of her free Tuesdays—the Tuesday after the bad news of Peggy's delayed recovery—Will took her to meet his mother in Lubbock.

Aurora met Will at the shop. She wanted to make certain everything was set for the day's business before she left. She also wanted Will to see all the improvements she'd made in such a short time—the very improvements he'd told her were a waste of time.

Will took his hat off and ran his fingers through his hair. It hardly looked like the same shop he remembered. Carpets had been shampooed, shelves dusted and polished until they gleamed with the increased overhead lighting.

Racks were shifted, new merchandise added, and displays updated. How could she have accomplished so much so quickly?

"Wow. This is still Raphael's Cards and Gifts, isn't it?"

Her heart swelled with pleasure at the admiration she saw reflected in his face. There also was the sweet revenge of showing him how wrong he had been about her efforts. "We just replaced burned-out fluorescent lights, and did some cleaning and rearranging. And we brought in some new goods. What do you think?"

"It's unbelievable. You must have a fairy wand hidden somewhere." He knew he had misjudged her ability to work wonders in so short a time. Even Peggy would want to keep these changes.

"No, just a lot of elbow grease and determination."

Will's reaction boosted her morale immeasurably. She hated to admit even to herself just how much his opinion mattered. After their argument about them, she became even more determined to prove her business acumen to him. His look of pleasure—and, yes, pride—in her accomplishments made her spirits soar.

He leaned near her ear. "Did I actually see Mattie smile and ask that customer to come back again soon?"

She raised her eyebrows and nodded. "Believe me, changing her attitude was much harder than the cleaning."

"Well, I don't know where you've hidden the cape and costume, but I am now convinced you're Wonder Woman."

She picked up her handbag and took his arm. Perhaps she could face meeting his mother after all. "Shall we go?"

Aurora sat on the passenger side of the large gray Chrysler, brushing off imaginary lint and straightening her blouse. She had resisted this meeting for as long as she gracefully could evade it. Meeting his mother seemed too personal somehow, too much like a commitment.

She still thought it a mistake, but she would just make it very clear that she was a temporary part of Will's life. *Think of this as a holiday from work,* she thought. *A day on the town will do you good as a reward for all your hard work in the shop. Sure. A mother is a mother and this is her only son,* she reminded herself, and brushed at her skirt once more. *Don't kid yourself. You are on inspection here, big time.*

"Relax, Aurora." Will noticed that she was as perfectly groomed and nervous as a schoolgirl on her first date, and looked so glorious today.

Aurora clasped her hands in her lap. "I know I'm fidgeting, Will. I don't know why I'm on edge."

Will gave her another appraising look. "I don't either. You look perfect to me." He longed to pull the car into some wayside and kiss her perfect mouth.

A faint blush crept into Aurora's cheeks as the car stopped in front of a new group of one-story condominiums in an upscale area of Lubbock.

Aurora took a deep breath before she left the car. The walk led to a closed gate of filigreed wrought iron. Will opened the gate and ushered her into a small, beautifully landscaped courtyard. As he did so, the front door of the condominium opened and a woman resembling Rose Webster stood in the shaded open doorway.

Once the woman stepped further into the sunlight of the portico, Aurora realized that the resemblance to Rose was fleeting and only superficial. The height and bone structure were the same, but there the resemblance ended. This woman had almost silver hair, and a merry face that showed years of laugh lines.

"Welcome, Aurora. My, I've heard so much about you,

but you're even prettier than I'd imagined. Come in and let's get acquainted."

Actually, Aurora wasn't sure what sort of person she expected Will's mother would be, but the bubbly enthusiasm of this woman came as a definite surprise. "Thank you for letting me come, Mrs. Harrison."

"Oh, no, no. You must call me Vivian. Now, I'm forgetting my manners. Would you like something to drink or a snack before we set out to see Lubbock?"

"No, thank you, um, Vivian."

"It's so lucky that you're here to take charge of Peggy's business, Aurora. Oh, my, what a lovely name you have. That shop needed someone to revitalize it. I hear that you've already improved it. Who knows what you'll be able to accomplish there in time?"

Aurora looked at Will, who seemed very busy looking innocent. To Vivian, she said, "Oh, didn't Will tell you? I'm only helping out until Peggy's well again and then I'll be looking for something similar to purchase on my own."

Vivian smiled and patted Aurora's arm as she would a small child's. "Yes, dear, Will told me all about that."

Aurora thought it best to change the subject. "This is a lovely home, uh, Vivian. I can see where Will got his love of antiques."

Vivian brightened even more, if that were possible. "These are mostly things from the family—Will's father's family as well as mine—so they all have a great deal of sentimental value to me. Come, let me give you a tour before we leave."

Each room held something special but the color schemes spoke of decades gone by. Will trailed along as Vivian went into detail. He managed to have his hand at Aurora's back, or his arm around her shoulders a great deal of the time.

Each time Aurora thought she cleverly evaded his proprietary gestures, he tried a new tactic. How could a man on crutches manage to have his hands everywhere?

There were family photographs on one wall. Aurora studied them while Vivian rattled on about each one. Several photos of Will reminded Vivian of his escapades as a young boy and made Aurora laugh again and again. What a handful he must have been.

"Just wait until your mother shows me your old photos," he threatened under his breath to Aurora as his lips brushed her hair.

"I hope it never happens," Aurora said primly. "It's bad enough to have my folks asking about you every time I call." She meant her comment as a reprimand, but instead Will looked pleased.

At one end of the room were the photos of Will and Nancy, some with Kelly included. Vivian paused in her dialogue.

"Nancy was such a sweet girl, and everyone loved her. We were all just crushed when we lost her." She patted Aurora's hand. "I'm so glad Will has found you now."

Aurora wondered what Will had told his mother and gave him a questioning look. The look was wasted on Will, who now occupied himself examining a book he had picked up from a table. No one could be as innocent as he tried to appear. Vivian moved them on to the next room as if they were small children she was herding on a school field trip.

Vivian's bedroom vibrated in red, white and blue. It included a white and brass bed and an antique dressing table which had belonged to Vivian's grandmother. "I just love cheerful colors, don't you?"

Before Aurora could answer, Vivian launched into a description of the quilt on the quilt rack at the foot of the bed.

"My great-grandmother began working on that quilt when she was only twelve. It was made from the scraps of the family clothing."

Aurora thought it a restful part of the most colorful bedroom she had ever seen. "It's really lovely, but not as, um, cheerful as the rest of the room."

"Well, they all wore mostly drab clothing then, you see. She had to use bits of cloth left from their sewing or pieces from clothes that had worn out. It was the first quilt she made by herself. The pattern is called Ocean Wave."

Vivian stopped in front of a group of pictures of a man at varying ages. Aurora knew this must be Will's father. They stood in front of the largest of the photographs. It must have been made about the time he died, for he seemed older in that portrait than in any of the other photos. The resemblance startled her. This is how Will would look in thirty years or so.

"This is my Riley, Will's father." She sighed, and a fond smile lighted her face. "What a dear man. I guess you can see the resemblance to Will. Riley loved ranching so much. He always was a good provider, too—and proud of it."

Vivian gave a conspiratorial chuckle and nudged Aurora. "Of course, the money from the oil wells didn't hurt us, but we'd have been just fine without them. Oh, but it near broke his heart when we had to move into Lubbock."

She turned and laughed. "After we'd been here a while, he found he loved this place too. What fun we had! Oh, I do miss him so." She touched her finger to her lips and then to the face on the portrait in front of her.

"Now Will takes care of all those details his father used to handle for me. I just don't have to worry about a thing, not one little thing. He manages my finances for me and helps me make any major decisions I have to make."

Aurora gave Will a frown. She'd bet anything that was what he did for Nancy, and would like to do for her. Well, she could handle her own finances and decisions very well, thank you. *But do you always want to handle them alone?* said a small voice.

Will placed his hand at Aurora's back and moved it in a small circle like a caress as he moved near. He looked at his mother with fond tolerance. "Are you ready to go out now?"

"Oh, of course. Just let me powder my nose and get my handbag."

Vivian kept them entertained for the rest of the afternoon with a lively tour of Lubbock, until Will begged for mercy. His mother only relented after she had extracted a promise from Aurora to return.

On the way back to Post, Will asked, "Well, were you surprised?"

"Yes." Aurora struggled for a tactful answer. "I thought she would be more like Rose, you know, sort of reserved and dignified."

Will laughed. "Then you were definitely very surprised."

"I really like her, Will. I meant every word when I told her I enjoyed the day. She's a lovely woman." Aurora looked thoughtful. "I can see why someone that outgoing would prefer city living. She just loves being with people, doesn't she?"

"Yes." Will hastened to prevent a false impression. "I hope you didn't misunderstand me when I told you she preferred the city to the isolation of ranch life. She never seemed unhappy while I grew up. In fact, she's always seemed happy regardless of her situation. It's just that I think she must be happier in a city. You could really see it when my father was still alive and they had friends around them every day."

"He wasn't confined to bed, then?"

"Dad? No, he just had to take life easy. They played bridge with friends, or took little trips, or went out to eat— nothing strenuous, but something every day. At least, it seemed that way to me."

"She doesn't come to the ranch much now, does she?"

"No, hardly ever. She prefers us to visit her. I have to admit Lori Beth is better at that than I am. Mom has so many activities here she hates to miss."

"It sounds like a nice life." As if thinking aloud, Aurora added, "I would think she would miss the quiet and beauty of the ranch, though."

Will smiled to himself and fell silent. When they reached Rose's house, dusk had given way to dark. Will made no attempt to get out of the car, but lowered the electronic car windows before he turned off the engine. The smell of the honeysuckle and Lebanon cedars drifted in through the open car windows.

Will seemed lost in thought for a few minutes. "Nancy loved the smell of honeysuckle. We always meant to plant some by the patio at the ranch."

The sound of Nancy's name on his lips startled Aurora. The love in his voice as he spoke her name wrenched at Aurora's heart. "You're still very much in love with her."

It wasn't an accusation, just a statement. She said it simply, but it suddenly meant the earth to her. A terrible sadness gripped her. There was no way she could fight a memory. Especially a memory of a woman he had truly loved.

Will looked at her, a mixture of sadness and compassion in his eyes. "If you're asking if I still love her, then I have to say yes. A part of me will always love her. Nancy was a good woman, a wonderful wife and a wonderful mother. She'll always have a part of my heart. Aurora, you must realize there's plenty of room still left there for you."

He wanted to make her understand. "We started dating when we were sixteen. Nancy was a big part of my life for a lot of years, but when she died—well, I thought my life ended when hers did. I realize now that life must move forward, and my life began to do that the day I met you."

She didn't know how to respond, so she sat in the twilight looking down at her hands folded in her lap.

Will seemed suddenly restless or impatient. He cupped her chin with his hand and turned her face up to let her eyes meet his. He looked very serious.

"I think it's time for us to talk about this, Aurora. You've been here long enough now to know what this area is like. You've met most of my family, and you've spent a little time with Kelly and me. And I've introduced you to many of my friends and the townspeople. By now you know what life in a small town is like."

"That's true." She waited expectantly for him to follow up this statement.

"Well, what do you think?"

"I . . . I like it here, Will. I like it a lot, and I like Kelly . . . and Rose, and the rest of your family and friends."

"More importantly, how do you feel about me?" Before she could answer, Will continued, "You must know by now that I want you to stay. That first weekend you were at the ranch I told you that I didn't intend to let you out of my life. Now, well . . . I want you to marry me so we can be together for the rest of our lives. Don't you see that I love you and I don't want to lose you?"

All she could think about was the affectionate tone of his

voice as he spoke Nancy's name. He still loves her so much, she thought. Even after three years.

"Oh, Will, I . . . I had all these plans, and now, I just don't know what to do." Aurora put her hand to her forehead. "I promised myself after my former fiancé dumped me that I would take some time to rebuild my life slowly and carefully and have my own business. Something that no one could ever take away from me. I had everything all mapped out. I wanted to travel, and . . ."

Will interrupted. "Look, Aurora, I love you and need you with me. I want us to share the rest of our lives together."

Aurora's plea was heartfelt. "Will, please give me a little more time." If only I could be sure he can love me as much as he still loves Nancy, she thought wistfully.

Disappointment and despair shaded Will's voice. His face looked grim, but his words were quiet. "All right, Aurora. If that's what you want. It seems to me that if you love me, you'll want to spend the rest of your life here with me as much as I want you to."

"There's more to it than that, Will. There's the love you still feel for Nancy. How can I measure up to her? How can I compete with someone who's no longer here? And—and there's so much more to consider."

Will looked at her as if he couldn't bear to hear what she said to him. "No, Aurora, there's not. I told you there's room in my heart for both of you. Either you love me and want to stay here with me as my wife, or you don't. Yes or no shouldn't be too hard to say."

"Please, Will, try to understand." Aurora placed her hand on his arm. In that moment she knew what her heart wanted. She wanted this man. How could she give up everything she had worked so hard for? When it came right down to it, Will only wanted to have things his way. And she would never be happy with him if that were true. She studied his resolute face, and realized that she didn't know what to say.

Will sighed.

"I am trying, but I'm finding it hard. I can give you more time, Aurora, but it's hard for me. Very hard."

Chapter Eleven

Aurora slipped inside the house and locked the door behind her. Sounds of laughter came from the television in Rose's room at the back of the house. The ache in her own heart would not allow her to face the woman she now thought of as a friend. She slipped up the stairs without even calling a good night to Rose.

Once in her room, she threw herself across the bed and cried as if there were no end to her tears. She wakened about midnight, her clothes hopelessly wrinkled and the bed linens in a twisted jumble.

This would never do. She was not some pathetic wimp, ready to give up on herself and the man she had to admit she loved. Perhaps she was making a mistake, but she vowed then and there she would make this her home and Will her life's partner. At least she would give it her best shot.

She no longer needed to travel further to find her destiny. This little town held all she needed for happiness. All she had to do now was make certain she took advantage of the opportunity life had presented her.

Yet how would she fight the love Will still felt for Nancy? She loved his loyalty and steadfast nature, and could not fault him for keeping the promises he had made to love and cherish the woman he married first. No. She only had to be certain he could love her as much as he loved Nancy.

With a flick, Aurora turned on the lamp beside the bed. She had to think this through. Back and forth she paced.

When her legs would hold her no longer, she threw herself into the rocking chair beside the window. It was there she sat as the first pale rays of dawn appeared in the eastern sky.

A shower revived some of her energy but did nothing to remove the dark circles under her bleary eyes. She tidied the room and hurried through her morning routine. Her mind whirled with plans ready to be implemented. She could hardly wait to get to work. The world was hers for the asking.

Will sat at the breakfast table and looked at his now empty plate. It looked as if it had once held eggs and bacon, but he had no memory of having eaten.

Kelly watched him suspiciously. "You don't look so good, Daddy. Are you sick?"

He made a disgusted harrumph. "No, not exactly."

Concern clouded her soft brown eyes. "Didn't you and Aurora have a nice time with Grandma?"

"Sure, honey. You know everyone enjoys Grandma."

When he told Aurora that Kelly was ten going on thirty, he had spoken the truth. Somehow the little girl always saw through him with adult eyes.

"I guess you had a fight, huh? Don't worry, Daddy. You and Aurora will get married and make babies and I'll have brothers and sisters. We're going to be a wonderful family, you'll see."

He sighed. It didn't look that way to him right now. "Maybe not. I sort of made a mess of things last night. I've been trying to think of a way to make up for it."

She came around to hug his neck and planted a big kiss on his cheek. "You'll think of something. I know she wants to stay with us. Then I'll have a new mother and brothers and sisters. You'll see."

Will wished he could be as certain as his daughter. "Maybe we should show her more about our life here. We always visit her in Post or have her here just for dinner or some special event. Let's show her the ranch—let's spend the day here with no one else to distract her. You only met her a few times, pumpkin."

"Yeah, but I really, really liked her," Kelly said vehemently.

His daughter began to dance around the room. "You know what? We could ride and she could see me on Misty. She's never gone on a trail ride with us."

"That's right. She never has." Will hoped a day with just the three of them together would give him another chance to convince Aurora she belonged here with him. He hadn't brought Kelly into it for a very good reason: he didn't want his little girl to be disappointed if things didn't work out.

Though he'd vowed to himself not to mention Nancy to Aurora until he proved his love for her and she felt secure with him, he could not forget the plans they had made for this house. People had thought a young couple foolish and extravagant to build such a large home so early in their married life. It was meant to be a home bustling with the laughter of children, a home sturdy enough to last generations.

Now he very much wanted those children to be his and Aurora's, wanted to see their children bring grandchildren here. God willing, he'd find a way to convince her to share that dream.

Aurora sat at what she had come to think of as her desk in the office at the back of the store while she made out an order for merchandise. She found it hard to believe that it would be Father's Day in only two weeks.

Since the night she refused his proposal after their trip to visit his mother, Will had tried hard to give her space. She knew she had hurt him, but she hurt also. She had lost herself in thought about the current situation when a large hand set a small paper bag on the desk in front of her.

Will stood in the doorway, on his own two feet at last. Aurora leaned back in her chair to look up at the handsome cowboy in the doorway and a look of astonishment spread across her face. She leapt to her feet. "You're not on crutches! You got the cast off your leg."

Will held out his arms and pivoted slowly for inspection. In one hand he held a cane. "I get to replace the crutches with this cane, and the cast is replaced by an elasticized brace for a while."

She hugged him briefly. "That's wonderful, Will. You didn't say a word to me about getting the cast off."

"Nick wasn't certain until he saw me this morning. I tried not to get too hopeful, just in case."

"This is a wonderful gift—getting your cast off in time for your birthday party next week."

He took her hand and guided her to her desk. "I have some bad news, too. Two of my men found your blue Mustang. I'm afraid it's a total loss, including the things inside. The guys tried to retrieve your belongings, but they shouldn't have bothered."

She sat down. "Oh, no. By now I'd given up on the car but I guess I still hoped I could salvage some of my things."

"I'm sorry. I know losing everything is rough. This mud ruined everything. At least now the insurance company will settle the claim."

"Will you let the men know I appreciate their efforts? I guess a tow truck will have to get it out of your way."

"Believe me, even a tow truck couldn't get it out. If the

insurance adjustor wants to see your car, I think we'll have to let him use one of our horses."

Aurora remembered the paper bag he'd placed on her desk. "So this is to cheer me up, then." She peeked inside.

"Right, I didn't want you to shoot the messenger."

"Mm. This looks like those chunky chocolate chip and macadamia nut cookies I love." She took out a freshly-baked cookie and closed her eyes as she savored the taste of the treat. "Ahh. This is marvelous. I guess I won't shoot you, after all."

"Ahem. I hoped you'd share." Will put on the most pitiful expression he could summon up.

"Oh, you did, did you? Well, I guess I can spare *one* cookie." Aurora's green eyes flashed as she tossed her curls across her shoulders and held out the bag of cookies toward Will.

Will took one cookie and returned the bag to the desk before he pulled her to her feet. "You have a smear of chocolate," he said as he leaned near.

With her hands resting lightly on his arms, Aurora looked up at him. "Oh? Where?"

"Right here." Will leaned toward her and his tongue flicked at the imaginary spot on her lips before claiming them with his.

Aurora responded to his kiss with an intensity to match his. She pulled him closer and let him edge her further into the corner of the office while he kicked the door shut with his foot.

When at last she pulled away, Aurora rested her head on Will's chest. "I think that's Mrs. Barton out there. She lives near you and she saw what you just did. She's probably about to burst with disapproval."

Will gave a low chuckle. "You can bet on it. That

woman knows everything that goes on in the county."

Aurora grimaced. "It's that she has to tell everyone else what she knows, or worse, what she imagines, that worries me."

Will tugged Aurora to him again. "Aw, forget her. Is that the wonderful Emily you just hired who was waiting on the old biddy?"

"Yes, and please treat Emily with all due respect, Will. I'll really miss her when Mattie returns from her vacation."

"Talk Mattie into retiring and keep Emily." He nibbled on her neck between bites of cookie.

Aurora made a half-hearted attempt to dodge his advances. "I wish I could. She only wants to work to get extra money for her family vacation. She wants to be a stay-at-home mom until next year when her youngest child starts school." She stopped herself from saying anything more. She had almost said she would try to talk Emily into returning then.

Will met her glance as if he could read her mind. He smiled a slow, crooked smile. "I guess you're fortunate she's available now."

The smile disappeared. For a moment he hesitated, then took a step back. He looked so uncomfortable, she almost asked him what was wrong but he took a deep breath and shrugged.

"Okay, I'm ready to concede I was wrong about the shop and you making changes. I see now that you have made some lasting changes that even Peggy can't easily undo."

"Thank you, Will. That means a lot to me."

"Have you kept records comparing this month to the same month last year?"

Aurora turned to the laptop computer she had set up on the desk. Within seconds she had the spreadsheets printing.

Will shook his head. "I should have known before I even asked."

"Don't make fun of my organizational skills. This place may not be a gold mine, but it could generate a respectable income someday."

"You think this place can compete with the mall and the stores in Lubbock? That's not a long drive and a lot of people from around here even work there."

"Oh, I know. That's a battle in every small town, but some places cope very well." She picked up some catalogs and flipped through to several places she had marked. "There would have to be more changes, maybe add more home decor and gift items, enlarge the inventory, that sort of thing. I have no idea how much money Peggy had to invest, but if it were entirely up to me I would aggressively cultivate the possibilities here."

"Our Old Mill Trade Days bring a lot of traffic into Post. That must take away some of this shop's gift trade."

"Maybe a little, but it also brings in a lot of business. I think the shop gains far more than it loses that weekend."

He looked at the catalogs. This represented serious thought and planning on Aurora's part. "You've made some contingency plans, haven't you?"

The speculation in his eyes alarmed her. She didn't want anyone to know what kind of plans she had made, or talk about the ideas forming in her mind.

She shrugged. "It beats talking to Mattie and it keeps me in practice."

He laughed and the tension eased. "Kelly and I want to celebrate getting my cast off by taking you on a trail ride on your day off tomorrow. She can hardly wait to show you how Misty performs and has a nice gentle horse picked out for you to ride."

Aurora tried to remember the last time she had been on a horse. "I haven't ridden much in ten years. I'm not sure I'll be a very good riding partner, Will. But, I'm game if you are."

"Great." He kissed the top of her nose and grabbed another cookie from the bag. "I have to get back to the ranch but I'll see you in the morning."

On the way back from the bank, Aurora stopped by for her almost daily visit to Peggy at the nursing home. Peggy had become more open to changes at the shop. Sometimes Aurora even sensed a lack of interest in the details she shared about those changes.

Peggy pointed to the latest edition of the paper which lay in her lap. "By the way, I love the ads you've placed in the newspaper. Several of my visitors have mentioned them. I'm afraid that at first I doubted they would increase sales, but now I can see they created quite a lot of interest."

"Have you thought of stocking a few more choices in china and pottery? I think it would encourage brides from this area to register selections with you rather than at the stores in Lubbock."

"I did think about it, but the good china companies I spoke to wanted too much money to establish an account. Some required as much as ten thousand dollars before they would even consider taking orders from me."

"I've been doing some checking, and I'd like to leave you some figures on several companies you might not have considered." Aurora took a sheaf of papers from her handbag and placed them on Peggy's tray.

The two chatted a few minutes about the store and events around town. Aurora didn't want to overtire Peggy and stood to leave. Peggy suddenly looked very serious and put a restraining hand on her arm.

"You know, Aurora, I have to thank you again. For years I thought about nothing but the store night and day. I really believed it couldn't go on without me there every single day."

Aurora didn't know how to respond. Business had improved dramatically with her own recent changes. In fact, she'd made so many little adjustments that it seemed now almost like a different store. Customers often commented on the improvements. They particularly liked the way she had brightened and cleaned the place so that it had a fresh and welcoming atmosphere. Aurora couldn't tell any of this to Peggy, and tried to be noncommittal.

"Well, you know people ask about you every day. You have a lot of friends and loyal customers."

"That's lovely, isn't it? Still, I thought I would miss it more. Aurora, I'm very grateful to you for handling things for me. I'm just so surprised to find that I enjoy not having to worry about the store."

Chapter Twelve

Perfect weather greeted her on Tuesday morning. The omni-present wind calmed to a gentle breeze which cooled the sun's rays. A few clouds, fluffy as cotton candy, dotted the brilliant blue sky. No day could be more perfect for any outdoor summer activity.

Aurora hurried to change into her blue jeans and a blue and white gingham shirt, the only longsleeved shirt she had with her.

Kelly knocked on the door and peeked in. "Aren't you ready yet?"

"Almost. I just need some shoes. I guess I'll wear my Keds. Maybe the horse won't care."

Kelly crossed her arms and shook her head. It seemed impossible to her that a grown woman didn't own at least one pair of boots suitable for riding. "You should get some real boots. They're much better for the stirrups."

Aurora slipped the canvas shoes onto her feet and rapidly tied the laces. "Well, for today, sneakers will have to do. I'll try to get some real boots. But I've noticed that managing a store doesn't leave much time to shop at other stores." She gave her jeans one last tug over her socks and followed Kelly downstairs.

Rose waited at the foot of the stairs with a hat and a pair of riding gloves. "With your fair skin, you'll need this hat. The gloves will help, too, if you can stand them in this heat."

Aurora set the hat on her head and fastened it under her

chin. Rose stood in front of her and adjusted the tilt of the hat slightly and stood back to judge the effect. "Kelly has a hat similar to this one"—she gave Kelly a pat—"and she should wear her hat, too."

"I have it in the truck, Aunt Rose. I'll put it on when we get back in the truck and then Aurora and I will be twins."

Aurora checked herself in the entry mirror. The well-used hat gave her the appearance of a real cowgirl. Her face actually glowed. Unfortunately, the glow came from sunblock lotion.

"I've lathered my face and hands in sunblock, but the hat will help. Thank you, Rose. I envy women with skin like yours that tans. My skin goes from white to red and on to painful blisters within minutes in the sun."

She turned to Will and Kelly and curtsied. "I'm ready, kind sir and fair maiden."

Kelly thought that remark hilarious, but Will just gazed at her with open admiration. For a moment, she thought he would pull her into his arms in spite of the presence of Rose and Kelly. She put her hand through his arm and gave a gentle tug which set him in motion.

Kelly's chatter about her summer plans and stories of her horse filled the short drive to the ranch. Soon the stone entry pillars of the ranch were in view. Will drove through and bypassed the house to drive directly to the barns.

Kelly's manic mood had her hopping up and down with excitement before she abandoned the two slowpoke adults and ran into the barn. A gentle palomino mare named Honeycomb would be Aurora's horse for the day. Will always rode a large black gelding named Midnight. Kelly's horse Misty proved to be a frisky brown and white pony, and there was nothing misty about her coloring.

"Misty, Misty," Kelly cooed and fed her a few lumps of sugar.

Aurora watched the pony nuzzle Kelly with obvious devotion. "Well, Misty seems quite content with her name, so it must be a good one."

Will brought Honeycomb up to her. "Pat her on the nose to get used to her. She's a good horse and won't give you any trouble."

Unconvinced, Aurora stroked the velvet nose. She had seen Will demonstrate the horses he raised. "She's not one of your cutting horses who's going to turn sharply and leave me hanging in mid-air?"

He chuckled at the thought. "No, not this one. I promise. Come on, I'll hold her while you mount."

Aurora climbed into the saddle with moves she hoped were far more graceful than she felt. Will's hands lingered on her waist and leg after she was seated in the saddle.

"I want today to be very special. I want to share this part of my life with you. You'll get to see an aspect of ranch life that you haven't seen on other trips here."

He retrieved saddlebags and canteens from the barn where he and Kelly had placed them earlier in the day. He put his cane in the empty rifle scabbard hanging from his saddle. Soon, the trio made their way down to the creek.

Although Aurora felt sure she recognized the big cottonwood tree by the creek, Will pointed it out. "That's where you landed after your swim in the flood."

She could only reach the bottom branches of the old tree because of the added height the horse gave her. The water had been this high! Now the little stream trickled by, only a few inches deep and a few feet wide. What a change the storm had made.

"Kelly told me we would see this tree, so I brought a ribbon to decorate it."

Kelly hopped down out of the saddle and helped tie a bright red ribbon around the trunk of the tree.

Aurora admired their work from her horse. "If I thought it would have helped the tree, I would have brought some nice big plant food spikes to put into the ground around the roots."

Will brought his horse alongside hers. Their legs touched as he leaned over to brush a kiss on her lips. Because Kelly was still busy adjusting the ribbon, he added a second kiss and murmured, "We could have a plaque made. Engraved with *This is the tree that saved Aurora's life and gave Will a second chance to win her love.* Or something like that."

Aurora smiled, somewhat embarrassed.

Will led them away from the ranch buildings and the stream as they moved across the rolling pastures. Aurora and Kelly began a contest to identify the myriad of wildflowers blooming along the stream and edges of the grassland.

"The bluffs look so nice and green. Is that cedar growing on them?" Aurora asked. She saw none closer and wondered if it could be a trick of the light.

"Cedar, yuk." Kelly made a face as she spoke.

Will nodded. "Yeah, it's a real hassle to keep cedar, juniper, and the mesquite under control and out of the pastures. We have to fight them constantly. Otherwise, they'd cover the land and ruin the grazing."

"You mean the settlers had to clear the grasslands of all those trees?" The enormity of that task seemed impossible to Aurora.

"No, they're not native to this area. Those three trees

were inadvertently brought in by the early explorers and settlers. They've taken over ranchland in areas where ranchers let them stay. Although they're pretty, I consider them major pests."

They rode across the rolling pastures and down into one of the many ravines that cut through here. The beauty and variety of the landscapes she was seeing amazed Aurora. "Your land has almost every kind of terrain, doesn't it?"

Will beamed with pride as evident as the love he had for his land. This was what he wanted her to see, for the beauty here to lure her as it did him. Once again he pulled his mount alongside hers as they gazed across the surrounding land. She felt the pressure of his leg against hers as he spoke.

"This is a good ranch. We have to be careful we don't overgraze, though, the way some of the early ranchers did. The land is relatively fragile. There are the bluffs of the escarpment, the beaches of the little streams, the ravines, the hills, and the rolling prairie. It has everything. I can't think of anywhere I'd rather be."

He moved ahead and dismounted to open a gate blocking their access to a narrow road of sandy soil. Kelly led Aurora through the gate and they waited while Will led Midnight through the open space and closed the gate behind him.

Kelly explained, "We always leave a gate the way we found it. Since you're our guest today, you don't have to, but Daddy and I take turns with the gates."

Will led the other two by a small herd of some of the cattle he raised. He pointed out his favorite breeding bulls and their harems.

Aurora winked at Kelly and said, "So this is all there is to ranching, huh? You sit on the horse and let it do all the work while the grass grows to feed the cows. Then the cows and bulls just do what comes naturally to reproduce and the herd grows while you wait."

Kelly said, "Yeah, that's pretty much it. But, there are neat dances and parties, too. And the stock shows and cattlemen's association meetings. Daddy is always busy."

"Hmnn. It seems to me the only work the cowboys have is to keep their fences mended and gates closed."

Kelly nodded in agreement. "Well, there is the roundup at sale time, but that's just once a year."

Will pretended to be offended. "You have wounded me, ladies. Next time I have to nurse a sick animal all night, I'll give you a call to help. Or, maybe you'd like to help with vaccinations or some of the other more gruesome procedures?"

Kelly leaned toward Aurora and, in a stage whisper, said between cupped hands, "He means castrating the bulls. It is really awful. I sneaked out to see last year and I practically threw up."

Aurora made a face. "No wonder. Think how the bulls must feel."

Will found himself focusing on the way Aurora's curvy rump fit so nicely in her jeans and swayed and bounced in the saddle. Her breasts moved with the rhythm of the horse. Why hadn't someone told her to wear a sports bra? On second thought, this was much better. He felt himself harden and cautioned himself to remember his daughter was present.

The trio passed by hay meadows and other cattle, and Will briefly explained the organization of the ranch. He shared some of the plans he had for the future as they rode along—and some of his dreams.

"I wanted to raise cutting horses since I was a little kid. I always planned to have the greatest horses in the Southwest. Seven years ago, I started with just a few horses. Now that part of the ranch keeps my foreman Raul busy full time."

At each gate either he or Kelly opened and closed it again after they passed through. By now they were no longer on Will's land, but had traveled several miles away.

Aurora wiggled in her saddle. They had ridden for a long time. Her seat and legs were unaccustomed to the bouncing of the saddle. She had a strong suspicion she wouldn't be able to walk tomorrow. She abandoned that depressing thought to enjoy the moment.

Will really did look like the hero of a western movie. His broad shoulders and trim waist looked perfect for the part. He and his horse seemed to move as one. There was no doubt he was as much a part of this land as the hills and creeks and meadows.

He led off again and Kelly and Aurora tried to stay close enough to him to converse amiably without having to shout. After navigating several other gates, at last they arrived at a gate bearing a large chain and padlock. Will produced a set of keys from his pocket as he dismounted and opened the lock. He closed the gate behind them but didn't lock it. At the top of a nearby hill sat a small building all alone in the large pasture.

Aurora tried to guess the purpose of the structure. "You know, from here that looks like a tiny church."

Will smiled. "It is a tiny church. Around here it's called a cowboy cathedral."

She looked in all directions. Not even a farm house was in sight, though the highway could be seen far in the distance. "Here? In the middle of nowhere?"

"Yup. It's for cowboys who can't get into town to attend

church. It used to be open and unlocked all the time. But vandalism's been a problem, probably by a few local teens. Now it's locked except for special events—or a neighbor who borrows the keys."

"How sad. It's terrible that a few bad kids ruined such a nice tradition." Aurora processed this amazing information—how could vandalism be a problem so far away from the city? Perhaps life here was not quite as idyllic as it seemed.

Still, in general it did seem like a much healthier environment for anyone. Certainly Kelly seemed to be one of the most well-adjusted children she had met, but perhaps her fondness for the little girl played a part in forming her opinion. Even so, this seemed an ideal place for children to thrive.

Kelly moved her left hand from where it had rested on the pommel of her saddle to her stomach. She rubbed her belly and looked at her father. "Daddy, I'm hungry. When are we going to eat?"

"We'll eat under that tree and then look at the chapel." Will led them to a large tree standing several hundred yards from the chapel at the crest of the hill.

Aurora dismounted and almost fell. Her legs, unaccustomed to straddling a horse for hours, wobbled like rubber. Kelly and Will seemed unaffected and began setting up for their lunch.

"Remember how easy it is for us cowboys just to sit on a horse," Will taunted.

"It's getting off and walking that seems to be the problem," Aurora said as she helped Kelly spread a blanket on the ground beneath the shade of the old live oak tree. Will suggested that as their guest, she sit on the blanket.

Aurora's independent nature meant she opened her

mouth to argue with Will that she could certainly do her share, guest or no guest. Reality prevented the retort when she bent over to straighten the corner of the blanket and her protesting muscles resisted. Grateful to stretch out and remain immobile, she sat on the blanket with her legs stretched out in front of her while Kelly and Will set out their meal of ham sandwiches and chips.

Will held up a plastic sandwich bag of crushed tortilla chips. "Looks like the chips took a beating in the saddlebags, so we have tortilla crumbs. Sorry."

"They'll still taste the same, and those sandwiches look wonderful. I don't understand how sitting on a horse can make me so hungry. After all, the horse did all the work." Aurora heard her stomach rumble with hunger pangs. She removed her gloves and stuffed them into her pocket.

"We brought cookies and apples for dessert. I helped Lily make the cookies yesterday." Kelly held up three sandwich bags of chocolate chip cookies. The cookies had fared better than the chips and were unbroken, for the most part.

"And ate more of the dough than you cooked, I'll bet." Will winked at Aurora as he teased his daughter. "I think Lily has to double the recipe to have enough dough for cookies when you're around."

The lovely day made the picnic in the shade of the old live oak tree a memorable experience. Aurora enjoyed the banter between Kelly and Will and felt honored to be included in their circle of family.

How easy it was to be with the two of them. Already she imagined herself a part of this family. What would it be like to live this life each day?

She loved this man and she knew she would grow to love his little girl. She could no longer imagine her life without them. Managing Peggy's shop had fulfilled her in another way she also loved. Who would have imagined her to be a small town girl after all?

How fortunate she felt to have left Houston and then, quite unexpectedly, to have found this lovely place. This glorious land with all its dangers and beauty had captured her heart as well. She hugged her arms in delight at the wonderful gift life had presented to her and the beautiful day she shared with these two.

"This is a lovely picnic. I don't know when I've enjoyed one more." The triumphant look exchanged by her companions puzzled her, but she decided it must be her imagination. Aurora lay back on the blanket and sighed in bliss.

And being waited on hadn't made her feel guilty for not contributing her share. She realized with a pleasant shock that being taken care of and cosseted wasn't as bad as she had imagined. Her take-charge nature hadn't suffered from her relaxation and enjoyment of the afternoon.

Carpe diem. Her high school Latin teacher had taught her the phrase. Seize the day. How perfectly it fit today. Nothing which produced her current state of euphoria could be at all bad.

Kelly decided to look for arrowheads and wildflowers, and mounted her horse. "Stay close, Kelly," Will cautioned.

As Kelly and Misty thundered out of sight, Will lay beside Aurora. She started to sit up, but he pulled her down to meet his kiss. His hands found their way to her hair before they caressed her back.

As their kisses deepened, he pulled her closer and their positions reversed. He pressed against her and his hand caressed her breast. His leg slid between hers as his kisses moved across her cheek and down her neck.

The sound of galloping hooves made its way through

the fog that enshrouded her mind. "Will. Kelly's coming back."

He looked into her face, his brow furrowed in question. "I don't hear anything."

"I do." The sound of hooves grew louder.

Will rolled onto his back, and let an arm fall across his eyes. "Sorry. I was overcome by your charms."

She found his hand and held it in hers. "You have some pretty captivating charms yourself, cowboy. Fortunately, a little girl on a running horse makes more noise than a little girl alone."

Kelly rode up and dismounted, clutching a hastily picked bouquet of wildflowers, which she presented to a delighted Aurora.

The picnic over, the trio led the horses over to the chapel and tied them to the hitching rail in front of the chapel door. Will unlocked the padlock on the door and stood back for Aurora and Kelly to enter. The small room smelled musty from disuse. A table at the front held a wooden cross. Red plush seats for about forty people faced the table and cross. Aurora ran her finger over the velvety upholstered back of one of the seats.

"No expense spared. Those seats are from an old theater in Lubbock." Will sat in one and rested his cane on the seat beside him.

"When is the chapel used now?" Aurora again thought it a shame that such a picturesque building had to be locked away from the world.

"Cowboy poetry readings," Will watched Aurora carefully for her reaction to his next words, "and weddings. This is a perfect wedding chapel. It's quite a sight all decked out in big white bows and candlelight."

Kelly added, "And you should see the neat old white

carriage and white horses the Chapmans rent to the bride and groom. It's great."

Now that was subtle, she thought. She looked around. "Hmm, does this wonderful place have a bathroom?"

Will smiled mischievously. "Kelly, show Aurora the bathroom."

Kelly laughed as she took Aurora by the hand. "Come on, I'll show you." Kelly led the way outside and around to the side of the building near the back. "This is it."

While Aurora watched, surprised by the child's unselfconsciousness, Kelly unfastened her jeans, scooted jeans and panties down, then squatted near the ground.

Aurora felt out of her element and sighed with resignation. "Okay, I get it."

She looked warily in all directions. "Are you sure no one can see us here?"

"I'm sure." Kelly seemed quite comfortable with the situation. Aurora braced herself and followed Kelly's example, while the little girl looked away.

She almost giggled. Imagine what her corporate friends in Houston would think.

Aurora and Kelly finished their business and went back into the chapel. Will still sat, grinning when they returned. "Well, did you find the ladies' room?"

Aurora gave him a dirty look. "Very funny. Some things about the wild west are just a little too wild for me."

Will still chuckled to himself as he grabbed his cane and left to take his turn outside. When he returned, the trio left the chapel and Will locked up behind them.

The ride home took them by a slightly different, yet just as scenic, route. The first pinks, reds, and golds of a desert sunset tinted the western sky as the three rode back to the ranch complex. What a wonderful day this had been, she mused. She felt a profound sense of contentment as they rode around the back of Will's home.

Her reverie was cut short when she dismounted. Aurora was sure her legs were going to fold under her. This was far worse than at lunch time. She grabbed the pommel and walked stiffly with the horse.

Kelly looked at her in concern. "You're walking kind of funny. Are you okay?"

"No. Yes. Well, let's just say that muscles I never knew existed are complaining to me. I'll probably walk like an old, old woman all day tomorrow—if I can walk at all, that is."

Will dismounted to help Aurora. "You wait here while Kelly and I put away the horses."

She waved away his help and struggled up to the patio. Her legs felt as if they were still around a moving horse, and with a sigh of relief, she sank into the porch swing.

Chapter Thirteen

Soon, Will stepped from the back door carrying a couple of soft drinks balanced precariously on a tray while he used his cane to close the door and balance himself.

"Sorry. Guess I chose too long a ride for your first time in the saddle."

"I'll be fine. Anyway, I really enjoyed it. Even the lack of plumbing didn't spoil it."

Will still looked almost nervous, hesitant. "Kelly has gone to town with the Chapases for pizza and video games. Lily left us some apple pie. I thought you and I could relax here a while before I take you back to Rose's."

Her eyes widened at the implication. "Okay. Uh, that will be fine. I'll help you dish up the pie."

When they entered the house, she felt differently than the other times she had been here. This time no injuries limited her movement, and there was no energetic little girl to chaperone their every move. No aunt, no matter how tolerant, safeguarded their actions.

"Let's eat on the patio again, can we?" Their first dinner at sunset remained a prized memory. How wonderful now to have the opportunity to recreate the feeling of that evening.

"Sure. You cut the pie while I get the plates and forks."

They chose to eat in the porch swing, drinks waiting on one of the low tables at each end. The sunset in a cloudless sky lacked the drama of her first sunset here. Still, the radiant colors made her catch her breath.

"I can't get over this view. What a splendid way to end a day."

"It's different each evening. I never tire of it."

He set his glass on the table beside the swing and lay his arm across her shoulders. He told her about other rides they could take and rides he had taken.

As night enfolded them, he pulled her into his arms. His tender kisses grew more ardent and he gently guided her to her feet and led her into the house. As if in a trance, she followed him to the bedroom they had shared on her first weekend here.

Had that been only a few days ago or years? Everything had changed so much since then. It seemed as if her adult life had really begun in this room with this man.

The cautious thoughts which raced through her mind were abruptly quieted by Will's kiss. She forgot everything except how his kiss tasted, how wonderful she felt in his arms.

Then the kiss deepened, exploring, enticing. She felt herself falling into a vortex of ecstasy where only she and Will existed. His tongue probed her mouth and she responded.

He pulled her closer, pressing her against him. She felt the heated bulge of his desire against her. Unconsciously she swayed to rub against him. He moaned in ecstasy. Or was that her voice?

Her hands moved slowly from his back to his chest and the snaps of his shirt as his trembling fingers fumbled at the buttons of her blouse. Between fervent kisses, discarded clothing dropped in a pile at their feet.

Will jerked back the covers of the bed and lifted her to place her gently on the cool sheets. He stood beside the bed, his eyes aflame with passion as he stared down at her.

"Oh, Aurora, let me look at you. You're even more beautiful than I remembered. This is how I've wanted to see you, here in this room and this bed with me."

Her eyes feasted on his lean, muscular body and his manhood rigid with his need for her. He reached into the drawer of the nightstand and withdrew a foil package. Without speaking she took it from him. His eyes closed and he gasped with pleasure as she rolled the condom down over his erection.

Their limbs intertwined as their hands explored. His mouth found its way to her rosy nipple and she gasped with pleasure as she kneaded his shoulders with her hands. This time she knew the moan she heard was hers, a low primitive sound which startled her.

When his mouth moved to the other breast, she felt herself on the edge of sanity. How could she withstand such bliss? She realized she called his name only after he raised his head to look at her.

"Are you sure? There's no going back."

"Yes, oh, yes," she cried as she pulled his mouth to hers. His fingers caressed the slick center of her womanhood, as sensations of pure pleasure coursed through her body. She thought she would explode if he didn't enter her soon. She wanted to beg him for she could withstand this burning desire no longer.

Before Aurora could cry out again he was in her and their bodies melded, each attuned to the other. They climaxed together in passionate union as he spent himself within her.

Will lay back on the bed with his arms still around her. He placed a kiss gently on her cheek and nuzzled his face on her shoulder.

"I knew it would be this wonderful between us," he

whispered. "You know I've wanted you since I saw you that first day in Snyder." His hands caressed her and he softly kissed her hair.

She brought one of his hands to her mouth and kissed his palm before she pressed it to her cheek. "Oh, Will, I never knew it could be like this." She nestled into his arms, then suddenly raised her head. A terrible thought occurred to her.

"Will, how long does it take the Chapases to get pizza and play video games?"

"Not long enough," he sighed.

The two reluctantly donned their clothes and remade the bed. "I'll take you home now. If the house is dark, Raul and Lily will keep Kelly with them until I get back."

Back at his aunt's house, Will came around and helped Aurora out of the truck. She appreciated his assistance, but she no longer cared about aching muscles. Reluctant to have the evening end, he guided her to Rose's porch swing. She sat down slowly. Will joined her, cradling her against his chest.

"You'll be calling me a city dude if I don't get better at riding than this."

Will laughed again, and leaned his cane against the house. The evening breeze once again stirred through the honeysuckle and Lebanon cedar and wafted delicate scents to Will and Aurora. The mingled fragrance reminded her of Will's proposal on a similar night. Would he repeat his offer? She now thought herself ready to answer him—if he hadn't changed his mind.

Will pulled her gently to him and kissed her. When at last he spoke, she could hear the catch in his voice.

"Aurora, I know I made a mess of things last time. I

should never have talked so much about Nancy, but I wanted you to understand my feelings. I can't go on like this, though. I want you too much. Can't you see what you're doing to me?"

"Please tell me."

"Aw, Aurora. I love you. Can't you see that you're more important to me than any woman in the world? I can't promise to forget Nancy. But I do promise that what I shared with her has nothing to do with my love for you."

"Sometimes I can't help feeling you're comparing us in your mind, that you wish I were her."

Will turned her to him, one hand on each of her arms. "You can't be serious. Listen to me. I love you more than life itself. No one living or dead is more important to me than you are. Can't you see that?"

"Oh, Will. That's what I needed to hear. I love you so much." Aurora melted into Will's arms.

"Remember that first weekend when I told you I didn't plan to let you get away again? I loved you even then. Marry me soon. We can announce our plans at my birthday party next week."

"That sounds wonderful. Oh, Will, I'm so happy. This makes everything just perfect. Peggy wants to sell me her shop, but I was afraid to give her a definite answer. I didn't want to buy it if I couldn't be with you."

Will pulled away and gave her an incredulous look. "What do you mean? You don't have to own your own business. I'll take care of you. Honey, there's no need for that now that we're going to be married. Everything's changed."

She shook her head and met his gaze as she spoke firmly. "Not that. I still intend to have my own business. Being married won't change my mind about being able to support myself."

He still looked puzzled. "You won't need to. I make enough money for us both to live quite comfortably. And have a real family. Don't you want children?" He ran his fingers through his hair in distress.

"Of course I want children. I want lots and lots of children—and I want them to be your children. But that doesn't mean I can't be a businesswoman too." Aurora's expression was positively mulish, and Will was exasperated.

"Do you think I can't take care of you? Don't you trust me? Surely you don't think I'll keep you barefoot and pregnant and refuse you an allowance? I tell you, there's no need for you to work now. You can spend your time running the house and raising children." His tone of voice indicated the frustration he felt—and the anger rising within him.

She stroked his hand, placating him, forcing him to understand. "Will, I have to be able to take care of myself. It has nothing to do with trusting you. I know you're a generous man, and that you're very successful. It doesn't change the fact that I want my own business."

His anger erupted. "Why, for God's sake?"

"I prefer to have my own source of income, but it's more than that. I don't want to depend on anyone. I want to contribute my share, be my own person, not just be an extension of you. I need to feel that I'm doing that."

He shook his head, unable to comprehend how a proposal of marriage could have ever deteriorated into this squabble. "Keeping house and raising children is a big contribution. What could be more important than that?"

She took a deep breath, willing herself to remain calm. "Oh, Will, it's much more than that. I've planned this for years. I've saved and scrimped and worked long hours so I could one day own my own business. It's been my dream for as long as I can remember. When people I knew were buying fancy cars or taking luxury vacations with their bonuses and pay increases, I invested my money with this in mind."

Will's expression showed his lack of comprehension. "Look, I have money in the bank and I don't intend to go anywhere unless I take you with me. You can feel secure with me. There's no need for you to own a business to find that security."

She knew his patience was wearing thin. His anger and hurt seemed to have closed his ears and heart to her pleas for understanding. "Will, I know very well you wouldn't ever take advantage or cheat on me. Do you think I could love you this much if I thought otherwise?"

If only she could make him understand. "It's a lot like your decision to raise cutting horses. You didn't *need* that extra income. But it satisfied a dream you had for a long time. And this is something I worked toward for a long time. It's not an insult to your ability or integrity. Can't you see that?"

"No, I can't. I only see that you have no faith in me. If you can't trust me, then there's no future for us."

"It's not a matter of trust." She placed her hands on his arms, but he shrugged them off.

"Like hell! No wife of mine needs to work to feel secure. If you can't trust me, what chance do we have?" Will stood and reached for his cane.

Aurora stood, her back very straight. He wouldn't even try to understand her needs. "There's no need to get angry. Don't make me choose between you and my financial independence. Can't you see that would be splitting me in two? You'd be tearing me apart, making me choose one dream over another, when there's no reason I can't have both. I'll never let myself become dependent. I've seen what happens to women when they allow that to happen."

Will threw up his hands in surrender. "Okay. Let's forget it. I hope I'll see you at the party on Saturday. In the meantime, I'll give you all the time you need to consider whatever you have to." Will turned and sadly walked away.

Aurora sank back to the swing and put her head in her hands. She heard Will start the truck engine and drive away. Had she just made the worst mistake of her life? She knew she loved Will, but why couldn't he trust her enough to let her have her dreams? Why couldn't she trust herself and him enough to tell him so?

Maybe she was wrong to want both the shop *and* Will. Maybe she couldn't have it all.

Aurora reclined in the swing, deep in thought, her heart breaking. On the verge of tears, she considered her next move—if she had one. What else could she have said to make Will understand?

He seemed to doubt her ability to be both businesswoman and wife. Difficult though combining the two might be, many women managed. Her own mother had taught school and raised three children, and done both jobs well. Had he no faith in her?

In her heart she knew that the new life she had set out to find was here, in this little West Texas town. If she bought the shop from Peggy, she knew she would love owning it.

This community had everything she needed to be happy. And surely she had a right to her dreams. *I want to have my own business, be a part of the community, marry Will, and help him raise Kelly and have children of my own,* she thought. Was that too much to ask?

Aurora put her head in her hands and burst into tears. Judging from Will's behavior, she wasn't going to realize any of those dreams anytime soon. If ever.

Chapter Fourteen

Aurora worried over her decision for the next two days. It pained her deeply that neither Will nor Kelly had called her since she had argued with Will on Tuesday evening. What else do you expect, she asked herself.

She missed him. She missed his call every morning, his funny stories each evening. She missed his touch, his kisses. How could she have become so dependent on a man when she had vowed never to let that happen? She didn't need him to provide income for her, but she needed him to provide sustenance of another kind.

She felt empty, half a person. It must be true. He was the one meant to be her other half, the person who made her whole. Had she lost him forever?

Soon she would have to give Peggy an answer about the shop. Yet, how could she contemplate staying here without Will? She couldn't stand to see him if he no longer wanted her. And, she could never bear seeing him with someone else. Just the thought of him in the embrace of another woman made her feel physically ill.

Early Friday morning just after the shop opened, Aurora looked up from her desk to see Will in the doorway. He stood silently for a few seconds, his face a mask. Aurora's heart skipped a beat as she stood to greet him. She wanted to rush to his arms, have him hold her and tell her everything would be all right. She needed to feel his touch, know his love surrounded her.

Will looked unsure of himself. Did he think himself unwelcome? He opened his mouth once, closed it, then tried again.

"Aurora . . . I, um, my birthday's tomorrow."

She tilted her head, waiting for more. When nothing else followed, she offered a tremulous smile. "I—I remember. Your aunt Rose told me you'll be thirty-four."

"I'm still having the party and I want you to come." He fidgeted with the hat in his hands, with his cane. "Guests can dance or swim or just visit. No presents, of course, but all of my friends will be there."

"It sounds nice."

"It'll start about six. There'll be barbecue and all the trimmings."

"The shop closes at six. I wouldn't miss your party, Will, but I'll have to come a little late."

"Right. The shop." He looked agitated and unsure of himself. "Look, once and for all, will you forget about this shop and just marry me?"

"I can't forget about the shop."

"Why not? Explain it to me, Aurora. Make me under-stand." His eyes pleaded with a pain that wrenched her heart, but she couldn't give in.

"For one thing, I've given my word to do my very best with this shop until Peggy is well. Now that she wants to sell the business to me, I don't know what to do."

"And if I gave you any advice, you'd say I was trying to control you, or something like that," Will said bitterly.

"No, Will—"

"Look, Aurora, it's clear enough that you don't trust me. And if you can't, then there's no future for us."

She felt shock reverberate through her. No future? Could she have heard him correctly? He couldn't mean it. No. Surely, it was still his hurt pride speaking. She grabbed the back of her chair to steady herself. Her knees seemed to want to give way. She sank to the chair and shook her head. "Will, it's not a matter of trust."

"With me it is. If you want to see me again, you'll have to come to the ranch. I won't bother you here again. I hope to see you at the party and that you'll come to your senses."

How could he be so stubborn? How could he be willing to throw her love aside to force her to deny the fulfillment of her dreams? Aurora's temper flared. "I guess if you want to see me again, you'll have to come to this shop—or to Colorado."

"That'll be a cold day in hell," he said quietly.

Will turned and left the store without a backward glance. In spite of her anger, Aurora felt her world crash around her. This time the pain was so deep she couldn't even summon tears to release the ache.

By Friday evening she became so distracted that she kept losing track of Rose's conversation at dinner. When the two of them dined alone, they took their meals in the cheerful breakfast nook of the kitchen. On this evening the brightly decorated room did nothing to lift Aurora's drooping spirits.

Rose's attempts at conversation were also unsuccessful. "I went to see Peggy this morning. She raved about how pleased she is with the way you're managing the store."

"That's good to know." Aurora pushed the food on her plate around with a fork, but couldn't force herself to eat more than a few mouthfuls.

"The activity director at the nursing home was so pleased with the donation of the greeting cards you took by last week. Peggy especially asked me to tell you how pleased she is that you said they came from her."

Aurora looked at her plate. "That's nice, Rose."

"She said Mattie comes to see her almost every evening."

"Well, Mattie is a devoted employee," Aurora said diplomatically.

"Peggy mentioned also that she appreciated how many times you've dropped by the nursing home to visit and let her know what's going on at the store."

"That's nice." Aurora traced an invisible pattern on the table with her finger.

"You know, I'm surprised that Peggy wants to give up the shop, but now she sees it can function very well without her. She seems to be enjoying her convalescence, don't you think? She mentioned that she's asked you to buy the shop. I'm so pleased. I hope that means you're considering it and plan to stay here."

Aurora's finger was still busy beside her half finished plate of food. "Rose, when I stopped by this afternoon I told Peggy I want to buy her shop. We agreed on a price and she's having a lawyer draw up the papers. She's anxious to get the sale finalized. I think she'll move to Florida to be near her daughter."

"Why, that's wonderful! I can't think of anything better for this town. You'll make it a real success, I know. I'll bet my nephew is on cloud nine."

"Oh, I doubt it. It seems I may have made a mess where Will is concerned." She looked at the older woman through brimming tears.

Rose crossed around to the other side of the breakfast nook and pulled on Aurora's arm. "All right, march right into the living room, Aurora. We're going to talk about whatever it is that has you so upset."

Aurora let Rose lead her into the living room. She sat in the big blue chair near the fireplace, the one Will had occupied on her first night at Rose's. Now Rose positioned herself on the ottoman and looked at Aurora sympathetically. "All right, Aurora. This isn't like you at all. Can you tell me what's bothering you?"

"It's Will. We argued on Tuesday, and he hasn't called me all week. Kelly hasn't called me either. And then, this morning he came by the shop and we argued all over again. Will . . . Will wants me to marry him." Aurora looked at her lap as she spoke, apparently oblivious to the fact that she was mercilessly twisting the linen napkin she had absentmindedly carried with her from the kitchen.

"Is that what's upsetting to you? I had the impression you were—um—more than a little fond of my nephew," Rose said tactfully.

Aurora sighed and looked up. "Yes, of course I am. Oh, Rose, it's worse than that. I'm desperately in love with him. That's the problem. But I have to convince him I can be a businesswoman and a wife and mother simultaneously."

"I see. I thought there was tension recently. I'm ashamed to admit I even feared it might be the idea of raising another woman's daughter that caused you to hesitate with Will."

"No, oh no. You know I adore Kelly, too. You see, at first I was afraid maybe I was just the one who happened along when he decided to get back into circulation. You probably know more than I how much Kelly and Lori Beth wanted him to start dating."

Rose smiled. "Those two have been after him to date, especially this past year or so. But, dear, I'm afraid the rest of us were almost as bad."

"Well, I was afraid maybe he didn't really love me. I know how much he loved his wife. And, after all, I've only known him for six weeks."

Rose shook her head. "You have no idea how many women we've tried to match Will with in the past three years. He wasn't interested until he saw you, Aurora. Anyone who sees you two together can tell you're made for one another. But what's the problem now?"

"It's been a dream of mine since I was very young to have my own business. Well, Will doesn't want me to. He thinks I should just marry him. He can't understand that I want and need to be financially independent. He wants me to be a stay-at-home wife like Nancy and his mother and Lori Beth. I know that should be enough, but I need this business. I can't be Nancy all over again for him, even though she couldn't have loved him any more than I do. We argued about it. It was horrid, and just when things seemed so perfect."

She gulped back the tears that threatened to overflow. "Will said if I wanted to see him I would have to come to the ranch. I told him if he wanted to see me he would have to come to the shop, or later to Colorado." She tried to smile. "Wasn't that stupid of both of us?"

Maybe it would have been better if I'd never come here, never met him, she thought. No. This man is *the one* meant for me, I know that. She wasn't going to give him up without a fight.

"Remember when I first came? I had all those plans to travel before I settled down, give myself some time. Those plans seemed so important to me until I met Will. Now I can't imagine going anywhere without him."

Rose looked stunned and placed her hand to her cheek in a manner of dismay. "Oh, my dear, those words give me goose bumps."

Aurora gave her a puzzled look, so Rose continued. "Well, not the part about being engaged, but the part about travel sounded all too familiar."

Rose took a deep breath, as if bracing herself. "Aurora, I told you that the only man I ever really loved married someone else, but I didn't tell you why or who he was. The subject is still so painful that I never discuss it. But now I think I'd better make an exception for you—and for Will."

Rose stood and walked over to adjust something on the fireplace mantel and when she turned back to face Aurora there was pain on her face.

"I was so keen to travel and see the world before I settled down. I was in love with a man I had known all my life, you see. He was content to stay on his ranch forever, but I"— she threw her arms wide and her head back—"I wanted to see the world, experience all of life before I settled down to marriage. I kept putting him off. One spring, I decided I'd take this grand trip and booked a tour of Europe that lasted most of one summer. We had terrible arguments about it, but I left anyway."

Rose pounded her left hand with her right fist. "Oh, I was so certain that I was in the right, and that he was being selfish. I thought he didn't want to understand my needs."

She sighed. "Well, while on that trip I realized that I had been foolish. Oh, I missed him terribly. I realized it was I who had been selfish to expect him to just wait around indefinitely. I could hardly wait to get home to tell him." Rose sat down but not with her usual regal bearing.

It pained Aurora to see Rose so distraught. She had never before seen this elegant woman lose her composure. "What happened, Rose?"

Rose took a deep breath and straightened slightly. "When I got home, my parents came to the train to meet me. I wondered where my sister Vivian was, and asked.

Even though we're very different, Vivian and I have always been very close.

"I can still see the look my parents shared in uncomfortable silence. Finally, Mother said they had something to tell me."

She sighed and dropped her hands. "Well, you can guess. The only man I've ever loved was Riley Harrison, Will's father. He finally gave up waiting for me and married my sister Vivian."

Aurora reached for Rose and clasped her hand. "Oh, Rose, I'm so sorry. I didn't know."

She shrugged. "You've met my sister. She's very easy to love. She had never let me know how much she loved Riley, because she thought he and I would be married. When I left after Riley and I had quarreled, she thought it was really over between Riley and me. There's no way I could find fault with either Vivian or Riley. The only fault was mine."

"No wonder Will is your favorite." Now she understood why Will received such special treatment in this house.

"Yes, he's my favorite. I can't help it. He looks just like his father, you know. He even walks like him. The sound of his voice is the same. Yet, each time I see him, I'm reminded of my foolishness. I can't help thinking that if I had only been more understanding, Will could have been my son instead of Vivian's."

"And Will knows how you feel?"

A speculative look came into Rose's eyes. "I believe he does. I've never told him, of course. I've never spoken of my feelings to anyone but you, but he's dropped hints a few times that let me know he understands. He's always been very attentive to me—much as a son would be."

Rose leaned forward and took Aurora's hands in hers. "I don't want you thinking I'm unhappy or that I feel I've

155

wasted my life. I have had a good life and expect to continue doing so for many years. I guess the whole reason for this depressing story is to let you know just how much Will and Kelly mean to me."

"I know they do. I know also, that you mean as much to them." She understood now Will's treatment of Rose, his deferring to her wishes as if she were a second mother.

"He's a good man. He suffered a lot when Nancy died. He seemed to feel he should have been able to help her overcome the cancer that killed her. But he couldn't. He has this second chance for happiness now with you and I don't want to see his stubborn pride cause him to lose what I lost."

Rose patted Aurora's hands once more then stood. "There has to be a way you can work things out. It's a new idea to him, having a wife who works on her own. Be patient with him, dear. He's well worth the effort."

"Yes, I know that. I just don't know how to reach a compromise. I don't think I could bear seeing him and not having him love me. I know I could never be as brave as you and see him with another woman."

Aurora stood and said with firm resolve, "I won't give him up. I have to resolve this with Will. And the sooner, the better."

Chapter Fifteen

On Saturday, Aurora worried the entire day. There were more than the usual number of customers in the store choosing cards and gifts as well as those choosing something for Father's Day or a June wedding. Instead of feeling pleased by the increased business, she could concentrate on nothing but the impending party at Will's. She glanced at the clock a dozen times an hour.

As she rang up sales and talked to customers, her mind rambled to Will, his ranch, what she would say to him. Twice she made mistakes in ringing up sales. She told herself she was getting as bad as Mattie. Still, she could not keep her mind from Will. Each time someone with a gray Stetson passed by the store or entered, her heart leapt to her throat.

How could she convince him she loved him even though she had decided to buy Peggy's shop? How could she bear to part from him if she failed? If only she could see him again, maybe she could do a better job of explaining. If he still wanted her.

Before their argument—and before her world caved in—Aurora had blown a large part of her salary from the shop on clothes for this party. Quite unlike her, but she had assumed she'd be his date, and on inspection, so to speak. Although she knew many of his friends, there would be many more friends and relatives there she had never met.

With great care, she had chosen a long blue denim skirt, and found a western-cut blouse to match. Aurora knew the greens in the pattern of the blouse made her eyes look an even deeper green, a fact confirmed by both Rose and the sales clerk at the dress shop. At Rose's urging, Aurora splurged on a new silver necklace and earrings in a Zuni sun pattern.

She looked down at her feet and wished she had taken time to break in the new brown boots. They were beautifully tooled on the sides, but felt painfully stiff to her feet and ankles. Already her feet were tired from the unaccustomed weight of the boots, and she could not imagine dancing in them by evening. She only hoped she would still be standing. Maybe the new clothes would give her the confidence she needed to attend the party and to face Will tonight. If she decided to attend.

Why even pretend? She knew she would go. And if she could manage to see him alone she would make him understand. If he would talk to her.

Chapter Sixteen

Will stood at a massive barbecue wagon he had borrowed from a friend who used it for chuck wagon cookouts. He checked the meat once more. It was tender, juicy, and ready to serve.

Some of his guests were still swimming in the pool. A small western band set up under an awning on the sun deck played "Tennessee Waltz" for the few couples who danced on the patio. Other guests sat or stood about in small groups visiting with one another. Most guests also sent frequent glances at their host, and looked more than ready to devour their share of the barbecued meat and the multitude of other dishes prepared for the backyard party.

The strings of colorful Japanese lanterns and streamers of crepe paper seemed almost depressingly cheerful. He saw Kelly moping about under the lanterns. She'd been mad at him all week, and his housekeeper Lily had hardly given him a civil word. He supposed Kelly had given everyone the story on her dumb dad.

The laughter of his guests now sounded hollow because of the absence of a particular silvery laugh among them. What a fool he'd been! How had he let things get so out of control? How could he make sense out of this mess?

What would he say to Aurora when she came? *If* she came was more like it. He'd practiced his apology all afternoon. He'd tell her how much he loved her, how much Kelly loved her, how they needed her.

Surely she would come, he worried as he looked once

more at the watch on his wrist. Twenty minutes until seven, and still Aurora hadn't shown up.

He felt a knot ball up in his stomach. Maybe she wasn't coming. *You should have called and apologized,* he chastised himself. *You should have let Kelly call her. No, you should have gone to that damn shop this morning and apologized. Better to eat a little crow than have her out of your life, you dolt.*

Instead he had tried to punish her for her lack of faith in him, but he'd punished only himself. His stubbornness cost him far more than he bargained for. He'd lost the most important woman in his life. He stood, silently cursing himself, when his aunt approached.

Rose stopped beside Will, her brow furrowed in a worried frown. "I thought Aurora would be here by six-thirty, Will."

Will felt the knot growing. "I guess she's not coming," he said as casually as he could.

"Oh, of course she's coming. I helped her get everything ready this morning. She looked lovely. She had a new skirt and shirt to wear and some very handsome Zuni jewelry. Why, she even bought new boots to surprise Kelly."

Hope rose slowly in his heart. "Good. Maybe she changed her mind."

Rose placed her hand on his arm. "I know you two quarreled. In the past I've made it a policy never to interfere, but you were wrong about Aurora, dear. Take it from a career woman, Aurora's love for you is no less even though she wants her own business."

Rose's grip on his arm tightened and her voice pleaded. "Oh, Will, you know you're like a son to me. Please . . . don't let stubborn pride make you miss your chance at happiness. I missed mine with your father. Sometimes you don't get a second chance."

Her admission stunned him. Never in his thirty-four years had his aunt mentioned her love for his father. Although his mother had dropped a few inadvertent hints, as far as he knew neither of them had ever spoken of it to anyone. It must have cost his aunt a great deal to mention it now. It moved him so he could only whisper as he gave her a lingering hug, "I know, Rose. I know. Don't worry, I won't let Aurora get away. I love her too much."

Rose pulled away and patted his arm, her composure regained as she walked away. Only Will had seen that composure slip, only he had heard the long-ago pain in her voice.

Where was Aurora? My God, what if she had already left for Colorado? No, he calculated, Peggy couldn't come back to work yet. Aurora had promised to stay until Peggy could come back, and she was a woman of her word. Nor would she lie to him, he knew. If she'd said she loved him, then she meant it.

Will called Raul over, and asked him to start serving the guests. "But where will you be? You're the birthday boy."

"I have to eat some crow before I can eat the birthday dinner. I'll be back as soon as I can."

The foreman shook his head and smiled. "I hope eating this crow improves your disposition and gets Aurora and you back together. You, my friend, have not been worth the bullet it would take to shoot you for the past few days." Will nodded. He had to agree.

Will rushed through the house to the garage. He hoped he could get his car out and maneuver through the mass of vehicles parked in front of the house. He found both his car and truck solidly blocked.

In a frantic rush he looked for a familiar car to use. Maybe his mother's car or Rose's waited at the edge of the dozens of cars and trucks blocking his drive. But if he had to saddle Midnight, he would. He stopped short when he saw a familiar Jeep pull to a stop at the edge of the cars. His breath caught in his throat and time seemed to move in slow motion.

Aurora emerged from the Jeep, a small gift-wrapped package in her hand. When she saw him, she gave him a questioning half-smile. His feet seemed to be weighted with lead as he moved forward to meet her. He could hardly breathe.

Aurora was determined to remain calm and rational. She had practiced her speech carefully all the way out here from town. She saw Will walk toward her and tried to read the expression on his face. Thank God! At least he looked happy to see her.

She exhaled and realized she'd held her breath since she first saw him walk back and forth among the cars. She would be able to talk to him. She had another chance to make him understand.

"Hello, Will. Happy birthday." She stopped and asked tentatively, "Is something wrong? You looked as if you lost something."

"I almost did—the most important thing in my life." He stood in front of her, not touching her but his eyes caressed every part of her, memorized each feature.

He nodded at the gift. "Is that for me? I said no gifts, remember?"

"First, I have to say something." She stood very straight and started the speech she had practiced in the car. "It was very hard for me to come here tonight, but I have to say some things to you."

She took a deep breath and launched into her speech, searching his face for a sign of his reaction. "I want you to know that I agreed to buy the shop from Peggy. I intend to make it a very successful business, one I can be very proud of. I also want you to know that I . . . I love you very much, and I hope you can realize that and appreciate it."

She swallowed hard but kept going before she lost her courage. "I intend to be very much a part of your life to give you that opportunity. You'll see me every time you go to a social function, at church, at the homes of your friends.

"Will, I won't let you shut me out of your life as you have this past week. You'll see me every time you turn around. If you can't love me under these conditions, I still intend to stay here and make this my home. I still want to be friends with Kelly, and get to know her better. You are a part of me now, an important part of me. I don't want to lose you, to have you shut me out."

"Is it my turn yet?"

"No. I . . . I, um, yes. I guess that's all I have to say. It's your turn."

Will stepped toward her and put a hand on each of her arms. "Oh, Aurora. I don't care if you buy Peggy's shop. I don't care if you race cars, fly planes, or run for public office. For all I care, you can sit on the front porch and knit all day. I just want you with me."

He pulled her to him. How good she smelled, how wonderful she felt in his arms. In spite of his longing to sweep her off her feet and carry her to his bedroom, he pushed himself away to look into her eyes.

"I want to see you every day for the rest of my life. I want you beside me when I go to sleep each night and beside me when I awake the next morning. I want us to have children together, to have grandchildren and great-grandchildren around us. If your dream is to own your own business, then so be it. Will you marry me and live in my house with me and make it our home?"

Aurora threw her arms around Will. "Oh, yes. That's what I want, Will. Just love me as I am." If she had more to say, her words were smothered by Will's mouth on hers. When at last they broke their embrace, Will caressed her face. She reached her hand to his cheek. Tears of happiness shone in her eyes as she smiled up at him.

She held up a crumpled present, the recent victim of their embrace. "Don't you want to know what your present is?"

"It couldn't be better than the one I just had." He took the small gift from her and unwrapped it. Inside lay a key attached to a red enameled heart. He looked puzzled.

"It's the key to Peggy's shop. No—I mean, it's the key to *my* shop. You already have the one to my heart."

He held the key and chain with the dangling heart as if it were a treasure of inestimable value. "Yours is the only one I need. But thank you for this one too. I'll treasure them both."

Raul came searching for his friend. "Hey, your guests are asking for the guest of honor. They sent me to see what's keeping you. Now I know."

Will looked as if he would burst with happiness. "I had a very special birthday present waiting for me."

The foreman looked from Will to Aurora. He clapped Will on the shoulder. "From the look of the two of you, I'd say it looks more like an engagement gift here than a birthday gift. Ah, perhaps you'll be making an important announcement to your guests tonight, no? My friends, what a great party this will be!"

About the Author

In addition to being a mom to two delightful daughters, *Caroline Clemmons* has experience that includes working as a newspaper reporter and columnist, an assistant to the managing editor of a professional psychology journal, and as a bookkeeper for the local tax assessor-collector. Caroline and her husband are living happily ever after on five acres in Parker County, Texas, where she is now able to write full time.